*To Carole
Enjoy!*

Sheila Caldwell

Changed Days

Sheila Caldwell

Published by New Generation Publishing in 2021

Copyright © Sheila Caldwell 2021

Cover illustration from an encaustic painting by Sheila Caldwell

First Edition

The author asserts the moral right under the Copyright, Designs and Patents Act 1988 to be identified as the author of this work.

All Rights reserved. No part of this publication may be reproduced, stored in a retrieval system or transmitted, in any form or by any means without the prior consent of the author, nor be otherwise circulated in any form of binding or cover other than that which it is published and without a similar condition being imposed on the subsequent purchaser.

ISBN   978-1-80369-129-9

www.newgeneration-publishing.com
New Generation Publishing

Previous books by Sheila Caldwell

An A – Z for Lightworkers
Chosen

Poetry Pamphlets

Words on the Wing
Melange

Contents

A New Start 1

The Pink Shawl 13

Lace Dowry 20

Aunt Maddy 29

Retribution 36

The Visitor 41

May Magic 60

The Group 66

Maggie Balfour 69

Sorry Missus 80

Nosey Neighbour 86

Vikings 89

Travelling Light 92

Too Little Too Late 96

Sunday's Child 103

The Laundry 109

Café Dreams 175

Foreword

This collection of short stories does not follow a theme. It is a complete mixture of tales; some light-hearted, others sad or serious. Some are based in truth while others are totally fictitious. There are stories set in the distant past and others that are up to date, but they have one thing in common – the characters involved all experience a change.

A New Start

Jane felt her excitement rise as the first stirring bars from the church organ sounded, and the small congregation rustled to their feet and turned in her direction.

'Well, lass, here we go,' said her father hoarsely, taking her arm. 'Your mum would have been so proud.'

Jane nodded, unable to answer. Mixed emotions filled her heart as she and her father made their way amid the soft light of candles towards the altar decorated with lilies and white lilacs. *Look at the flowers. Take in every detail.* Handing her small bouquet to Amy, she turned towards Michael. He gave her a tremulous smile.

'Dearly Beloved, we are gathered here together....' began the minister, but Jane could hardly take it in. She glanced at her fiancé through her lacy veil and realised that he was shaking. *Poor darling, he is so nervous*. Reaching for his hand, she gave it a reassuring squeeze, then suddenly Michael turned and blurted out, 'Sorry - I...I can't do this.'

Jane stared after him, unable to believe it as he fled up the aisle, and barged through the doors. The last thing she remembered was the scent of flowers as her knees gave way and she sank into the arms of her bridesmaid.

It was over eighteen months since that day, and Jane was replaying the events in her head for the thousandth time. She recalled the short letter of apology which had arrived after the wedding date.

'Dearest Jane,
I am so sorry. I love you but I am married and have two children here in Ireland. I hope you can find it in your heart to forgive me.
Michael.'

Jane sighed as she remembered the whirlwind romance with the handsome salesman who'd said he had no family; her happiness on discovering her pregnancy just before the wedding; her mixed emotions when she later miscarried. Everyone said she'd had a lucky escape. Michael could have been jailed for bigamy. Finding the hurt and humiliation too much, she'd returned to stay with her father.

The strident ring of her doorbell brought her back to the present and she hurried to tug open the stiff front door. She was expecting the friend who had been her bridesmaid.

Sure enough, Marjorie stood on the doorstep holding a beautiful bouquet of chrysanthemums which she placed in Jane's hands while she wiped her feet on the doormat.

'Oh, it's so good to see you!' she squealed and hugged her friend.

'And you too,' answered Jane, warmly. 'Come in, come in to my new abode. I'm afraid there are still packing cases everywhere but I'm gradually getting organised. Give me your things.'

Having shrugged out of her warm coat, Marjorie stuffed her gloves in the pockets and handed it over to Jane. She walked over to the log burner.

'This is so welcoming,' she remarked as she warmed her hands. 'How are you keeping now?' The question was asked a little hesitantly. 'I only saw you briefly a few days after the wedding…er…fiasco … and then, again at your father's funeral.' She touched her friend's arm. 'And of course, you had the sadness of the miscarriage in between.'

'Well, I'm slowly getting back to normal, whatever that is.' She straightened up, 'I'll just stick these flowers in the sink meantime, then put the kettle on and we'll have a catch-up. Sit yourself down – I've cleared us a space - and I'll just be a minute.'

She bustled off to the kitchen, returning shortly with mugs of tea and a plate of biscuits. 'Help yourself, Marj. How are *you* doing?'

'Oh, I'm fine. Still working at the office. We miss you, you know.'

'That's nice, but I won't be going back there. Too many memories.'

They drank their tea in silence for a few moments.

'I'm so sorry that it has taken me so long to get in touch with you again, Marj, but I feel I've just been in a haze over the past months.

You know … Michael, then losing the baby … and then my father's death. It was a terrible shock when he had the car accident.'

'It must have been awful. He was such a lovely man.'

'Yes, he was,' and she sighed. 'It has been some year, but I'm doing my best to move forward. Dad left me comfortably off.' She munched on a biscuit. 'I sold his house and my flat, and that's enabled me to move here to this pretty village.'

'It certainly looks like a good place to live and I look forward to seeing around your lovely house.'

'Sure thing. But I warn you, there are boxes and bags like these everywhere,' she indicated with a sweep of her hand around the room. 'I just brought everything from both houses and haven't had the inclination yet to start sorting it all out. But I will, soon,' and she gave a nod of conviction.

'I'm sure you will,' nodded Marjorie in agreement.

'I just closed all the doors on the stuff, and I've been living between the kitchen and my bedroom. I've thrown myself into grappling with the overgrown garden. I feel that doing that has somehow helped me to heal from the hurt and grief.'

'I'm sure it has.' Marjorie sipped her tea. 'I thought your front garden looked very neat.'

'Oh, come and look out at the back garden. I have a vegetable patch and an orchard as well as a lawn and cottage garden. Plenty to keep me occupied.'

The moved over to the window and Marjorie exclaimed with delight at the beautiful view. 'Oh, I love the way you've allowed the flowers to grow naturally in your border by the wall! All higgledy piggledy colours, but tall flowers at the back and lovely clumps of low plants at the edges.'

'Well, a lot of them were already there, and I've just let them seed themselves. It's a case of keeping them all in check. Most of them are nearly past now that it's getting colder.'

'It looks like you've had lots of vegetables growing down there as well, and oh, a pretty wrought-iron seat in front of your fruit trees.'

Jane smiled. 'We can have a wander in the garden after our cuppa, if you like. You can take home some apples.'

'Oh, that would be grand. Anyway, let's get on with our chat.'

The two friends spent a pleasant afternoon catching up with each other.

'My life has been like a bad Country and Western song,' Jane exclaimed to her cats Pepper and Millie, who were comfortably ensconced on a sofa piled with cushions. They kept their counsel and merely blinked. 'This place would be paradise to collectors and dealers. Where do I begin?'

She looked around at the disparate assortment of items. Tables and chairs, chests of drawers, packing cases still filled with books and ornaments, pictures, lamps and vases which jostled for position with boxes spilling over with bedding and towels. 'I'd better make a start somewhere, I suppose', she sighed. 'Jane Henderson, spinster of the parish, get a grip and stop feeling sorry for yourself! Remember, How do you eat an elephant? One bite at a time!'

Her self-admonishment was cut short by a ringing at the doorbell and a continuous clack-clack of the letterbox. Letting out a breath of annoyance, she clambered over the obstacles and managed to wrench open the stiff, rarely-used front door, to find herself looking down into the eyes of a little girl of about seven and a boy around five. 'What do you want?' she snapped, disgruntled at the interruption.

The children took a step back, then the girl straightened her shoulders and said, 'Our kite has got stuck in one of your trees. Daddy sent us to ask if it was alright if he came to get it? He's bringing his ladder.'

'Oh, is he indeed. Well, I don't like strangers in my garden and...'

'Oh, look, Iona, she's got a pussy-cat!' yelled the little boy as Pepper sidled past Jane's ankles to see what was going on. 'Oh, there's another one in the hall,' he squealed excitedly and pushed past her to pet Millie who encouraged his attentions.

'Does your Mummy not teach you any manners?' Jane retorted.

'My Mummy's dead,' he answered matter-of-factly. 'She died when I was born. We've just moved into our new house here. Daddy sent us out to play with our kite. He's unpacking. Have you just moved here too? What a lot of stuff you have!' he prattled on. His sister tried in vain to hush him.

'I..I think you'd better go and show your father where the kite is,' Jane stammered, feeling uncomfortable.

'Can we come back again to play with the cats … please?' the small boy enquired with a winning smile.

'I..I suppose so,' Jane found herself saying.

She heard the gate clicking and the children ran off to meet their father while Jane hurriedly closed the door and leaned against it. She wasn't ready to talk to people, and especially not a *man.* That little boy had thrown her. 'I wish I hadn't spoken so harshly,' she murmured. 'Poor kids with no mother.' She watched the proceedings in her orchard from behind the curtains and breathed a sigh of relief when they all left.

It was two days later on a cold November afternoon when the letterbox was rattled again, and the pair were standing smiling on the doorstep. This time, she wasn't quite so annoyed. In fact, if she was honest, she was pleased to see the children.

'Hello, lady,' piped the boy, can we see the pussy-cats?

'Please,' nudged his sister, reminding him.

'Please?'

Jane smiled. 'We...ell,' pretending to consider,' as you've asked politely, you may come in.'

They both stepped into the hallway expectantly.

'I think we should have some introductions, don't you?' and without waiting for an answer said, 'My name is Miss Henderson, but you may call me Jane. And you are?'

'I'm Iona, and this is Arran,' the girl divulged.

'Nice names,' said Jane as she divested them of coats and boots and showed them into the living room where they went in search of Pepper and Millie. Jane had made some headway with the clearing out and although the room was comfortable, there were still boxes in a neat pile under the window and numerous black bags piled in the hallway labelled, CHARITY SHOP and RECYCLE. The children spent some time cuddling with the cats, then Iona looked around and asked, 'Why do you have all these bags and boxes, Jane?'

'Oh, I'm having a massive clear-out. Most of these things belonged to my Mummy and Daddy who are now dead, sadly, so I'm sorting through everything and deciding what to keep and what to sell or recycle or give away.'

Iona thought about this for a moment or two then said, 'Could I help you? Daddy says I'm very good at tidying and organising.'

'I'm good at tidying and or'nising too', chipped in Arran, not to be left out.

So, despite any misgivings, Jane soon had the children involved putting things in bags and stacking books in the bookshelves. They were having some hot blackcurrant and biscuits when the doorbell rang.

'Oh, dear, I think that might be your Daddy, come to see where you are,' said Jane, hurrying to the door.

'I hope these two scamps haven't been in your way,' smiled a tall, kind-looking man holding a large umbrella against the sleet. 'I told them just to visit for a short while as I'm sure you'll be busy with Christmas coming up, Mrs....?

'It's Miss, and please call me Jane,' she answered feeling awkward and not wanting to meet his eyes, 'and your children have been no trouble, they've been helping me sort out some things.' She didn't invite him in and he stood dripping on the doorstep.

'Come on, kids, time to go, and I'm David, by the way', grinned the man, and he waited while the children pulled on their boots and got bundled into their coats and hats.

'Thank you for having us,' chorused the two youngsters.

'Please come anytime, 'Jane heard herself say.

"Bye, Jane, 'bye Pepper, 'bye Millie,' they called.

'Well, well, I think we were a hit, don't you?' Jane nodded to the cats, then realised that she was grinning for the first time in months.

Next day, Jane remembered David mentioning that Christmas was coming. She hadn't even given that a thought. Last Christmas had been spent hiding under her duvet. 'I'm going to get back into the world', she suddenly announced to herself. 'I saw packs of Christmas cards somewhere that Dad had bought. Where were they?' She rummaged in her desk drawer. Having found the cards and her address book and pen, she settled down in front of the fire to write to the friends she had left out of her life.

Every few days. Iona and Arran called round. Sometimes they just stayed for a short while playing with Pepper and Millie. At other times, they would help Jane empty some boxes and enjoyed hearing her reminiscing about the contents. Iona loved to look at books and try on jewellery and Arran liked the telescope and binoculars which had belonged to Jane's father.

It was Christmas Eve before Jane knew it and she'd received cards and invitations from many of her good friends.

Sitting with the cats by the fire, the clack-clack of the letterbox alerted her that Arran was probably on the doorstep. Heaving the cats from her lap, she hurried to the door, to be met by Iona, Arran and David.

'We wish you a Merry Christmas, we wish you a Merry Christmas, we wish you a Merry Christmas and a Happy New Year,' they carolled, laughing.

'We are off to my parents for Christmas, but thought we'd just call in to see you before we go,' explained David.

'Oh, that's nice of you,' murmured Jane, and she smiled at the group. 'Would you like to come in?' she ushered, stepping aside.

'Yes, please. We've got something for you,' whispered Arran.

Iona was carrying a large biscuit tin importantly and hurried into the living room. 'This is for you.' stated Arran proudly and handed over a colourful, home-made card.

Jane looked at the picture on the front and felt a blush rise to her cheeks. There was a drawing of three figures labelled, Daddy, Arran and Iona and beside them was a figure labelled, Jane, plus two fat blobs labelled, Peper and Mili. Glitter had been liberally sprinkled over all, and lots of XXX's. 'It's b..beautiful,' she stammered. 'It's the best card I've ever had.'

The children beamed. 'Now you must look in the tin,' Iona ordered pointing to the box.

Jane lifted the lid and uncovered mince pies, somewhat misshapen but lovingly decorated with pastry stars and Christmas tree shapes.

'We made them,' said Arran standing tall.

'Daddy put them in the oven', confessed Iona, 'but we cut out the pastry and spooned in the mincemeat.'

'They look delicious. Shall we have some now?' asked Jane.

'I'm afraid we'll have to be off, as we have quite a long car journey,' apologised David, ' but we'd like you to come to us on New Year's Eve for a party. I thought I'd invite some neighbours so we can all get to know each other. I expect you already know everyone.'

'Actually … I hardly know anyone yet. I've been a bit of a hermit.' And to her own surprise, Jane heard herself say, 'I'd love to come, thank you.'

The children squealed with delight and both of them hugged her and jumped up and down.

'They just adore you,' David acknowledged, 'and I've really appreciated the time you've spent with them recently. As a journalist I had a deadline to meet, so although I work from home, it was good that the kids were occupied with some adult company when I was busiest.' He indicated to the children that they must go.

'Hold on just a sec,' said Jane, and ran upstairs. She came back down with two gift bags with tissue paper stuffed in the tops.

'This one is for you,' she said handing a small, gold bag to Iona, ' and this one is for you,' as she handed a larger one to Arran. 'Not to be opened until tomorrow morning.'

'Thank you, thank you,' they chorused, holding their packages tightly.

'Come round and see me when you get back,' Jane called as they set off down the path. 'Merry Christmas'.

She stood watching the happy group and waved until they disappeared in the car. She'd given Iona a little bracelet, and Arran had her father's binoculars.

'I think life is getting better,' smiled Jane to the cats, who purred in agreement.

The Pink Shawl

'Mm, the Faerie Glen sounds intriguing, and the turn-off for the track should be next on the left,' Jenny stated, looking at the map. The side road appeared as predicted and Callum turned off the main road on to a rough track winding beside a loch.

'It's so beautiful here.' sighed Jenny. 'Oh, look, there's a gate ahead. How odd.' There was indeed a gate across the road barring the way, with a notice which said, SOUND HORN FOR GATEKEEPER. An old cottage stood on the left with roses climbing around the door and tumbling over the fence.

Callum complied with the request, and a woman appeared and walked towards them, unfastened the latch and pulled open the heavy, five bar gate. Lowering his window, Callum smiled and thanked her. She nodded and came over to the car.

'How far to the Faerie Glen? ' asked Callum.

'Oh, it's just a mile or so ahead,' she answered, glancing at Rosie gurgling in her car seat. 'What a beautiful baby you have there. Keep a close eye on her. You wouldn't want to lose her.'

She turned back towards the gate. 'Not today,' she added in an undertone.

'Don't worry, we'll look after her, 'Callum answered as he drove past.

'You'd better,' muttered the gatekeeper to herself as she watched them disappear. 'It's Midsummer's Eve on a seventh year.'

'I wonder what she meant, ' frowned Jenny. 'Why would we lose Rosie? I thought she looked rather odd and old fashioned, and did you see the colour of her eyes? I've never seen such a bright green before.'

Callum nodded. 'Now that you mention it, she was a bit unusual, with that long skirt. Such strange material. Anyway, let's not allow anything to spoil our day out, eh?' He started to whistle to himself and Jenny relaxed, feeling her spirits rise again.

. . .

'Wow, isn't this just perfect!' exclaimed Callum. They both stepped out of the car into the sunshine and gazed around at the water. The trees cast dappled sunlight on the grass.

'No wonder it's called the Faerie Glen,' laughed Jenny. 'You can just imagine fairies around all those wild flowers, and elves sitting on that mossy bank. Let's lift Rosie out and get our picnic started.'

She busied herself laying out their picnic rug and settling Rosie in the shade of a rocky outcrop. 'I'll feed you in a moment, gorgeous, and then you can have your nap. Would you bring out the bags, darling?'

Callum helped to gather everything they needed from the car and Rosie was soon enjoying her feed.

'I'll just change her and settle her for a sleep, then we can relax and have *our* lunch,' said Jenny with a smile. Afterwards, she laid Rosie down on the rug. 'It's a bit warm to cover her ... oh, I know, I have my pink pashmina shawl in the car. That will be lighter, just in case she gets a draught,' she fussed.

Half an hour later, Rosie was asleep and Jenny and Callum lay back in the sun, luxuriating in the warmth and peace.

'Isn't this an idyllic spot?' murmured Jenny, listening to the gentle gurgle of water in the nearby burn. 'Perhaps Rosie would like to have her toes dipped when she wakens.'

'What a good idea. I think I'll have a paddle myself right now,' laughed Callum, removing his shoes and socks and rolling up his jeans. 'Are you coming?'

'No, I'm just going to relax here and watch you,' replied Jenny.

She leaned back against the rock and smiled as Callum sat on the banking, splashing his feet like a small boy. Looking lazily around, she was surprised to see a large clump of blaeberries growing behind the rocks. 'Callum, I'm just going to pick some berries over here. They're early this year.'

Callum nodded and gave her a wave. She glanced over at the sleeping Rosie then moved a few steps away to pick the tiny dark blaeberries. The sun was warm and she spent a happy ten minutes or so filling a sandwich box, then walked back around the rock to the picnic spot.

At the place where she'd left Rosie peacefully sleeping, she saw only the pink shawl lying on the ground. Her eyes darted to where Callum was still sitting by the burn, expecting to see him holding the child, but no, he had his face upturned to the sun, eyes closed. As panic rose, she started to shake, and nearing hysteria, heard herself scream, 'Rosie, Rosie, where are you? Callum, Callum, help, Rosie's gone!'

Callum leapt to his feet and rushed to her side. They ran about searching and calling in vain, alternately sobbing and blaming each other for leaving her. There was no sign of anyone in the vicinity. Hands shaking, Callum tried to call the police, but there was no mobile signal in the remote glen. He shoved his feet into his shoes.

'What'll we do? Shall I leave you here and try to get some help?'

'Yes...oh ... no, don't leave me. Oh, I can't think straight!' sobbed Jenny, her eyes streaming.

With reluctance and apprehension, they packed up and Callum drove back along the road. 'We can try to phone again when we get to the gatekeeper's cottage. Not far now. I...I just can't believe this is happening.' Shaking his head, he squeezed Jenny's hand. She sat staring ahead, dishevelled from tramping through heather and bracken, shoulders slumped, face swollen and wet with tears, clutching the pink shawl to her chest.

They turned the corner that had previously brought them to the gate. There was only an ancient ruin with just a gable-end standing. A tree was growing in the centre, with brambles and gorse all around, and a grey stump of wood where the gatepost had once been. Where was the pretty cottage with roses round the door and the flower-filled garden?

Callum and Jenny stared. *Were they going mad*? *Had they gone through some time warp*? Jenny let out a wail of despair.

This time, Callum managed to use his phone. 'Our baby's been ... stolen,' he gasped, his mouth dry with fear, and blurted out the story to the police. Saying the words aloud confirmed the reality. In a daze, he assured Jenny that help would be with them as soon as possible.

. . .

'I left my baby lying here, lying here, a-lying here, I left my baby lying here, to go and gather blaeberries.' Seven years later, Jenny sang the old Scots song quietly to herself as she made her annual pilgrimage to the glen. 'How apt. Someone else must have had the same experience. *Hovan, Hovan Gorry og O, I've lost my darling baby O,'* she sang softly, patting the pink shawl wrapped loosely around her shoulders. 'And that's not all. I lost my darling Callum, my marriage, my friends ... my whole life,' she murmured aloud to no-one, remembering the hounding from the media, allegations of murder and the hate mail. 'Even after the case was dropped, everyone thought we must be insane. They wouldn't believe us about the house and the gatekeeper. Even our best friends.' Jenny shook her head as she spoke aloud, reliving the pain.

She glanced down at the posy of white rosebuds lying on the passenger seat. The memories played over in her mind. 'I was neither use nor ornament,' thought Jenny with a sigh. 'I spent my days hiding in bed crying, and my nights, walking the floor; just lurching from one day to the next in a haze of despair and medication. Friends eventually left me to get on with it. No wonder Callum couldn't take any more! Then the poor guy lost his job. Oh well ... at least he is happy now with his new wife ... and child.'

Her eyes were misted with tears when she stalled the car - shocked from her reverie by the blurred sight of the gatekeeper.

The flower covered cottage was back.

The woman pulled the heavy gate over and stepped forward. 'Would you like to meet your daughter?' she invited, a hand gesturing towards the opening.

Jenny couldn't speak. She just stared and nodded.

'Every seven years, it is our custom to steal a Human and take it to our kingdom. It learns about the wonderful work of creation carried out by the faerie folk.'

'Do... do they come b...back?' stuttered Jenny.

'No. They continue to live and work in our realms which they prefer. They eventually become spirit, like us. It is small recompense for all the destruction that you Humans do to the natural world.'

Jenny stared into the strange, green eyes.

The gatekeeper continued. 'It is usually an infant we take as that is easier to procure, but if an adult comes willingly, that will suffice.' She waved the car on.

Jenny was bewildered. She drove jerkily to the former picnic place and stumbled from the car remembering to grab the posy. Immediately, a cleft opened in the rocks and a dazzling light shone out along with the beguiling sound of distant music. Through the brilliance stepped a pretty young girl. She was the image of Jenny herself as a child. *Could it be? Was it possible?* 'Rosie, is that you?' she whispered, stepping forward.

The child nodded shyly and accepted the roses being offered with a smile. Beckoning to her mother, she turned towards the light.

. . .

A few hours later, some ramblers found the abandoned car with no trace of the owner; just a pink shawl lying beside the rocks.

Lace Dowry

'What do you mean you're getting married to this...this *woman*?' blurted Louiza, flinging out her hand and glaring at me. I'd just been introduced, and Nik had broken the news. 'What's wrong with the nice girls here? You could have your choice from Chryssa, Katerina, Zoe, Maria…'

'Enough Mother,' Nik cut in. 'You are being hurtful to Allena. We've made our decision anyway, ' he said taking my hand, his eyes full of love. 'We're getting married in six months.'

She took a sharp intake of breath. 'Are you a good cook?' she flung at me.

'I…I can get by, I'm sure.' I replied.

'I haven't had any cause to complain,' said Nik, giving my arm a squeeze.

'What about sewing. Can you make clothes and curtains and bedding?'

'I've never sewn since school, but I can learn if necessary.'

'If necessary indeed! Of course it's necessary.' She threw up her eyes. 'And what about the lace dowry? I don't suppose you can make lace either?'

'I don't know anything about a lace dowry,' I answered, looking to Nik for help.'

'All brides on Zakynthos try to bring up to a hundred pieces of lace and embroidered linen which they've gathered over the years, to the marriage. This is their traditional dowry.

Sometimes their mothers help out,' she retorted, before Nik could get a word in.

'Well, Allena is from mainland Greece, and the tradition has died out there,' Nik said in my defence. 'We thought you would be happy that we were getting married *here* so the family won't have to travel to Athens.'

'Oh, Nikolas,' she cried, 'she can't cook, she can't sew, she doesn't have lace and she's an *incomer*,' she reeled off, marking off the supposed faults on her fingers. Throwing her apron over her face, she sat down and wailed as though she'd just had a bereavement.

*

That was years ago. Nik was working as an engineer in Athens and I met him when he was brought into the hospital where I was completing my nursing training. He had acute appendicitis and I happened to be working on men's surgical at the time. We both felt an immediate attraction, and over the course of his stay, we got to know each other well. After he was discharged, he contacted me and we started dating, fell in love and consequently planned our wedding.

Both my parents had died three years earlier in a car accident and I had only one married sister. I lived in the nurses' home and mostly ate in the canteen. As Nik came from a larger family and was the youngest of four - a brother and two sisters - we thought it would be good to marry on his home island of Zakynthos. I made enquiries about transferring to the hospital in Zakynthos

Town as Nik had been offered a good job with a large engineering firm there.

We organised a trip with the intention of first breaking the news to Nik's family in their small village, and then looking for a suitable house in the main town. We wanted to surprise Nik's folks, but I hadn't expected such hostility and prejudice from his mother. It took her a few days to absorb that we were serious and fully intended marrying whether she liked it or not.

Nik's father, Marios, was quite different, thankfully, having given me a warm welcoming hug when he'd arrived home later. He owned a large olive grove, but apart from the harvest in November, he didn't really have a lot to do, but managed to 'have to tend to his olive trees' daily, and kept out of his wife's way. He was a kindly soul and stayed quietly in the background.

Mother-in-law came up with a plan to save her family's reputation. I recall her saying to me, 'We cannot have you coming into this family without your lace dowry, so I will personally make some pieces for you as you do not have your mother now. I have a good friend who is a wonderful lace maker and I'll pay her to make fifty articles for you. No-one needs to know that you didn't provide them yourself.'

It was good of her to make that offer, but I knew it was really to save her own face and was not given entirely out of generosity.

The week before the wedding, we had both moved back to Zakynthos, I to stay with Nik's sister Chara and her family, and Nik, with his parents. I was informed that we would be having a day when all my lace dowry would be on display in the parental home, along with the other wedding gifts received.

The day arrived and the house had been cleaned from top to bottom by Louiza, her two daughters and of course, me. I think most of the village turned up throughout the afternoon and evening. I knew Nik had been popular with the local girls and it was obvious that many were peeved that he was marrying away from tradition. When I talked to Nik about it afterwards, he reassured me.

'Yes, I've had some good times with girls around here, and I suppose it's only natural that they'd expect me to marry one of them, but it's *you* that I love and *you* I'm going to marry at the weekend.'

Around sixty pieces of lace and embroidery were draped and hung throughout two rooms along with a display of other wedding gifts of dishes and kitchen ware etc. Drink was flowing freely and a continual supply of snacks appeared from the kitchen with granddaughters acting as waitresses. Everyone was anxious to meet the 'incomer bride' and many of the villagers pinned gifts of money to the lace, which was kind. It soon became obvious that what was supposed to be a secret, regarding the lace dowry, was anything but! Louiza's friend had made it her business to let everyone know that *she* had made most of the lace items. Louiza however gave the appearance of being oblivious to this, and sat smiling with her guests whilst sipping her brandy.

'My, you are a wonderful lace maker,' smirked one girl.

'It must have taken you months to make these tablecloths,' said another, slyly.

'I don't know how you managed to produce all of this so quickly, and all by yourself too,' said a third, winking to her neighbour.

I just smiled and mumbled something unintelligible with eyes down, and directed them over to the wedding gifts table instead. It was humiliating to say the least.

Our wedding was financed largely by Nik's father who insisted that our savings should be put towards a house. Marios also honoured my wishes for a reasonably small wedding with only close family and friends. My sister and her husband and children plus a few of my friends made the journey from the mainland. The rest of the wedding party was made up of Nik's immediate family and close friends. Thankfully, it all went smoothly even if Nik's mother was coolly polite to my side.

After we were married, we were expected to have the lace in constant use all over the house at all times. It seemed bizarre to me. We had lace curtains and embroidered tablecloths, lace-edged sheets and pillowcases, lace bedspreads and cushion covers, lace chair back and arm covers, covers for small tables, tissue boxes and toilet rolls. If it could be covered, we had a lace cover for it - even the telephone!

My mother-in-law expected to see it all being used whenever she visited. At first, I complied with this to keep the peace but in later years it was completely impractical. We had two little children, a boy, Marios Alexandros named after our fathers and a baby girl, Sara Louiza after our mothers. (Mother-in-law wasn't pleased about her name being second, of course). I folded most of the precious lace items and stored them away in tissue paper for safekeeping. The next time Mother-in-law arrived for a visit with her long-suffering husband, there were ructions.

'What have you done with your lace?' was her opening utterance before even saying hello.

When I explained that I didn't want the little ones to dirty or damage it because it was so exquisite, she seemed to think this was just an excuse.

'I knew you never liked it! After all the trouble I took to help you keep face. Of course, we knew it was only a matter of time before you showed your true colours,' she sniffed, turning to her husband, 'didn't we Mario?' The poor man just shrugged uncomfortably, but gave me a little wink.

'Hmph! Come on Mario, we're going!' and she turned and stomped out.

Nik called after her, 'This is ridiculous, Mother. Allena has prepared a lovely meal.'

'I'm so sorry. You know what she's like. Speak soon,' said Marios with a sigh. 'Presents for the children,' he added, handing over two packages. He mouthed, 'Sorry,' to me and departed.

'Well!' exclaimed Nik.

I sighed. 'I don't know what all the fuss is about. I suppose we better go over tomorrow and grovel.'

When we arrived at the house the following day, Marios was standing outside the front door, smoking. He gave us both a hug and indicated to me to go in, while he stayed outside talking to Nik and young Marios.

Mother-in-law didn't hear me come in carrying Sara. She had her back to me as I entered the room and was talking on the phone.

'I was so angry. After all the trouble we went to.' There was a pause. 'I know… young people nowadays!' Another pause. 'However, she seems to be a good enough mother to my grandchildren… for an incomer.'

I had to smile.

Sara gave a small cry and Mother-in-law turned round, shocked. 'Must go, 'bye,' and she quickly hung up.

'I'm sorry, we didn't mean to startle you,' I said. 'I wanted to come over and apologise again for upsetting you. I really do like the lace, it's just that there's too much of it for our small flat, and I don't want it to get spoiled.'

Just then, Nik stuck his head round the door. 'Marios wants Dad and me to push him on the swing. Will you two be alright for five minutes?'

'Oh, I think we'll be alright,' Mother-in-law answered, giving me a sideways look and half-smile, 'if I can hold the lovely Sara Louiza, that is.'

I happily handed baby Sara over. 'I don't want to hurt your feelings.'

'Apology accepted. Why don't you put the kettle on Allena and we'll have some coffee when the others come in,' and she turned to sit down with her granddaughter. 'There's some juice in the fridge for little Marios.'

As I came back with a cafetiere and mugs, Nik came in and sank happily into the settee. 'Oh, good! Coffee. Dad is taking Marios for a walk in the olive grove to see the baby goats.'

Mother-in-law laid Sara down in one of the armchairs to sleep, and took over the pouring of the coffee.

I sat back and looked around the room. 'You still have lots of your own lacework, Mother-in-law. I hope I'll be able to pass on some of mine to Sara when she gets married,' I said fingering a particularly delicate cloth on the coffee table beside us. 'Did you make this?'

'Of course,' came the answer with a smug smile.

'What beautiful embroidery and such delicate stitching,' I said, hoping to keep in her good books.

I turned the corner over to admire the neat sewing and gasped as I saw the label. 'It says here, MADE IN CHINA.'

'Oh, I ...I must have made a mistake. Th...That must have been a present.'

'Aha! Found you out, Mother,' laughed Nik and he looked under a different piece of lacework. 'Oh, oh, here's another, MADE IN CHINA and another!' He winked to me. 'After all the fuss you've made to Allena about handmade lace and honouring local traditions, and you've been cheating all those years!'

His mother didn't know where to look and just pursed her mouth and waved her hand dismissively. 'Em, I think I hear noises at the gate. I'd better go and get the juice ready for little Marios.

Nik and I had to stifle our laughter as we shared a hug.

'I don't think we'll be hearing any more about lace,' he said.

I agreed, heaving a sigh of relief.

Aunt Maddy

I poured a coffee and handed the steaming mug to my friend.

'I thought you were going away for the weekend,' Anne stated as she added some milk to her drink. 'What happened?'

I hesitated and took a couple of sips from my own mug. 'Well, we *were* meant to be staying with my mad auntie, but that changed.'

Anne spluttered into her mug and grinned. 'Mad auntie! Why do you call her that?'

'Oh well, Dave started it, I suppose. Her name is Madeline and I've always known her as Aunt Maddy, but events yesterday have really made me agree with Dave.'

'Come on then, spill the beans. What happened?'

I opened a packet of chocolate biscuits and we each picked one and started to nibble while I thought.

'I think I should give you a bit of background about Aunt Maddy,' I said, after a few moments. 'She is my father's sister and is now in her late eighties. My father died when I was very young and my Mum was never well off. Once, when I was about eight years old, when we all lived in Devon, Aunt Maddy invited my Mum and I to stay with her for a long weekend. She was most eccentric and insisted that we could visit on condition that we brought all our own food and cooked it ourselves. She was not going to feed us.

Mum drove an old van at the time, so we took sleeping bags in case Auntie didn't want us to sleep in her house – which turned out to be correct – and a camping stove etc. I was too young to know all the ins and outs but I suppose my Mum wanted to keep on good terms with her husband's sister. Anyway, we ended up cooking sausages and beans on the primus stove, while Aunt Maddy would give Mum a lamb chop or suchlike to fry for her.'

'That's incredible!' Anne exclaimed. 'You mean she sat outside with you and even got your mum to cook her food, *and* had a chop while you ones had sausages?'

I nodded. 'That's nothing. Wait until you hear the rest.' I took another bite of biscuit and some coffee. I sighed and looked down into my mug. 'One day, she suggested that she take us to the local art gallery or museum, I can't remember which, and as we walked up a hill towards the place, we passed a greengrocer's with fruit and vegetables piled in boxes outside. Next to that was a bakery with wonderful cream cakes in the window. I gazed at the lovely meringues, doughnuts and eclairs. I'd never had a fresh cream cake in my life. Mum was a good plain baker and made scones and tea loaves but couldn't afford shop-bought cakes. Aunt Maddy saw me looking and said, 'I'll buy you a cream cake as a treat, on the way back.'

I was thrilled, as you can imagine.'

Anne nodded.

'After our cultural visit, I was so excited to be going back towards the wonderful bakery with the tempting array of delights. What would I choose? But ... Aunt Maddy walked right past and went into the greengrocer's shop. I was horrified. What could I say? In those days you didn't question adults the way children do now.'

'Absolutely,' Anne agreed. 'So, what did you do?'

'Well, I just couldn't say, 'What about my cake?' but I finally managed to come out with, 'Auntie, are we going back up the hill again?''

'Back up the hill?'

'Yes, you know... past the baker's shop.'

'Oh, yes, of course. I forgot. I said I'd get you a cream cake for a treat, didn't I?'

I sighed with relief. However, that was short-lived. She turned and picked up a bunch of fresh beetroot and said, 'Ah, beetroot. We'll have that for a treat instead. Much better for you than a cream cake.'

Anne gasped. 'Oh no! What a horrid thing to do to a little girl.'

'Yes, wasn't it. I still feel the shock and disappointment to this day,' I replied.

We finished our coffees in quiet contemplation.

'Wait 'til you hear this one, once I was older. Another unbelievable event happened when I was working as a restaurant manager. Aunt Maddy had commanded that I phone her each Monday at midday. 'You are my only niece,' she said, 'and It is your family duty to keep in good contact with me.' The restaurant was closed on Mondays, so that usually suited, but one day I was very busy with accounts and a traveller and various tasks, and I completely forgot to phone. Well, she phoned me later in the afternoon, demanding explanations. When I apologised and explained how tied-up I'd been, she just humphed and stated that I would be hearing from her solicitor!'

'Good grief! What was she going to do? Cut you out of her will?' Anne said jokingly.

'Yes, that's exactly what she did!'

'Oh, no!'

'Oh, yes. Within a few days, I had a letter stating that I had been removed from her will and would no longer be a beneficiary.'

Anne looked at me open-mouthed. 'B...but you didn't do anything wrong.'

'I know, but that let's you see what a strange person she is.'

'Well, I think you are an absolute saint! I would have dumped her years ago! Do you still keep in touch on a regular basis?'

'I phone her once a month, but not at a specific time. I go to visit her a couple of times a year. It is a long train journey and a taxi to her house from the station.'

'Why, when she is so unkind?' Anne shook her head.

'I suppose I feel that she is my only living relative and... I need to just accept that she has mental issues! Dave says I have an unnatural sense of duty!'

'Indeed. Especially as you are doing it out of kindness.' Anne replied. 'So, tell me, what happened yesterday. I can't imagine what she did this time to upset you so much.'

I sighed. 'Well, when I phoned her recently, she invited Dave and me to visit her for an overnight stay. She said she wanted to get to know Dave.' I made a face.

Anne gave me a quizzical look.

'Aunt Maddy didn't come to our wedding. I can't remember her reason now, and we married ten years ago, however, out of the blue, she decided she wanted to see us. We drove there and arrived in good time. I went into the village and chose some lovely lilies and delphiniums in a smart florist's, then went to the chocolate shop and bought her some handmade chocolates.'

'Lucky lady!' Anne declared.

'We pulled up the drive at her house but she didn't come out to greet us. I knocked on the front door, rang the bell and waited, but no-one came. I thought that in view of her age, perhaps she was a bit frailer than the last time I'd seen her, so I opened the door and called out her name. No answer. I laid the flowers and chocolates on the hall table and indicated to Dave that I'd look in the living room.'

'Did you think you might discover her body?' Anne clasped her hand over her mouth.

'Well, it did cross my mind, but I thought it more likely that she'd had to take the cat to the vet or something. There was no note there for us. Dave said he'd check the kitchen while I looked into the two bedrooms. The spare room was tidy and made up as though ready for us. Aunt Maddy's room was bathed in sunshine and her cat, obviously fine, was sleeping in a sunbeam on her quilt. She raised her head, gave me a disdainful look, stretched, yawned, turned around and curled up ready to sleep again. The next moment, Dave shouted from the kitchen, 'Carol, come and see this!'

'I hurried through and Dave pointed to a note stuck to the fridge door with sticky tape.

It said,

> GO AWAY
> I'VE CHANGED MY MIND
> I'M UP THE HILL WATCHING YOU THROUGH BINOCULARS
> AND I WON'T COME DOWN UNTIL YOU'VE GONE'

'Wha...' Anne's mouth hung open. She laughed. 'The crazy old bat was up a hill? *Watching* you? At her age?'

I nodded and found myself giggling too. 'I didn't see the funny side of it yesterday after a hundred-mile drive, but you've got to laugh. You couldn't make it up!'

'What did you do then?'

'Well, we rushed outside and gazed up the hill, trying to catch the glint of her binoculars. We thought we saw her, surrounded by sheep and gorse bushes but couldn't be sure.

Anne was laughing but saying, 'Oh, how awful. What a dreadful woman.'

'Dave sent some rude gestures in her direction and told me to get in the car.'

'I hope you didn't leave the presents for her!'

'Nope. I went back into the house, picked up the flowers and chocolates, slammed the door and left.

Author's note – Unlikely as it may seem, this is a completely true story which happened to my friend. Only the names have been changed.

Retribution

The storm was picking up as Jack rang home on his mobile phone. 'I'll be there soon, darling. I'm bringing us a curry so you don't have to think about cooking tonight. A bottle of red too, okay? '

'Hmm, sounds like you're trying to butter me up Jack,' Gail answered wearily.

'I've said I'm sorry a thousand times and I really mean it. It's just you and me Gail.' He laughed wryly to himself at the pun as he drove off in the high wind which buffeted the car and tossed branches into the road. Rain battered against the windscreen and rivulets were running down the gutters as drains overflowed.

'You just put your feet up and I'll bring through a tray,' Jack called from the kitchen.

'Oh, I could get used to this new you,' Gail replied happily, pulling over the footstool and placing a cushion at her back.

'Not for much longer,' muttered Jack under his breath as he unscrewed the cap from a small bottle and dropped some of the powdered contents into the wine, resealed the bottle and carefully tipped it back and forth. He sprinkled the rest of the powder over Gail's aromatic chicken tandoori, stirred it in and eased it on to a plate with the rice. 'Here we are then,' he said, smiling as he placed the tray gently on Gail's lap. 'Get stuck into that, and have a good glug of wine.' He dropped a kiss on her forehead. Opening the bottle, he filled a large glass for his wife and settled down beside her on the couch with his own plateful.

'Are you not having any wine?' she asked.

'No, remember I'm driving to the airport first thing?' he said with an apologetic grimace. 'I'll have to settle for some fizzy water.' They ate for a moment in silence. 'Sorry I have to leave on a Saturday.' He tilted his head in Gail's direction. 'I was looking forward to a quiet weekend with you but you know what it's like. Conferences, trade fairs. There's always something.' He forked some chicken into his mouth. 'Will you be alright?'

Gail looked at him then nodded. 'I've grown used to being on my own over the years,' she tossed down some wine, 'what with your conferences and trade fairs ... and your many little indiscretions.'

'Oh, come on. I thought we were fine again. I've told you that's all over.' He blew her a kiss.

Gail had eaten all of the meal and was on her second glass of wine, when she yawned and slurred, 'Thish wine mush be strong. I can ... hardly ... keep my ... ' and promptly slumped to one side.

Jack waited a few minutes to make sure she was asleep then removed her plate which he washed thoroughly, putting the remains of the wine with the glass on the bedside table. On his return to the sitting room, Gail was deeply unconscious and barely breathing.

'Good, everything is going to plan.'

Snapping on rubber gloves, he carried her to their bedroom and laid her on the bed. Taking her hands, he pressed her fingers around the caps of two empty bottles labelled temazepam and prozac - courtesy of pharmacist Caroline. He laid them beside the glass, with a typed note which read, *Dearest Jack, I'm so sorry. I can't cope with life any more. This is the only way. Forgive me. G x*

*

At 5 o'clock next morning, Jack rose from a fitful sleep on the couch. He quickly showered and dressed. His cases were in the car. The storm was still raging so he thought it best to allow an extra half hour for the journey to the airport. At 5.30 he braced himself to go once more into the bedroom. Gail was lying in exactly the same position. She was quite cold to the touch and her face had a waxen appearance which made her seem like a beautiful sculpture. He felt no remorse, just elation that at last he and Caroline could be together and begin their new life. Slamming the front door with a sense of finality, he ran out into the downpour, a frisson of excitement tingling through him. The cleaner would find Gail's body on Monday morning and by then, he and Caroline would be far away.

He'd failed to see the note stuck on the kitchen notice board. *Dear Mrs. Hammond, I'll come in early on Saturday morning about 8 instead of Monday, as Bert is getting out of hospital then and needs me at home. I should be in the following Monday as usual. I have my key. Mary.*

Jack slammed the car door and set off out of the driveway, his windscreen wipers on top speed. They barely coped with the deluge. Anxious to get away, he jammed his foot down and screeched round the corner gathering speed. Through the blur on the windscreen, he saw the fallen tree too late as he aquaplaned across the road.

*

At 7am, Caroline was starting to panic at the airport. *Where was he? Why didn't he answer his mobile? Had something gone wrong? Why had she agreed to get him the tablets?* In her anxiety, she rang his home number, shaking with fear. *Please don't let it be his wife!* The answering machine clicked, 'Hi, Jack here. Sorry I'm unable to take your call. Leave a message after'... Caroline just heard his voice but didn't make out the words. The airport was too noisy.

'Jack, it's Caroline. I'm waiting for you. What's happened? I can hardly hear you. Flights for San Francisco have been delayed due to high winds,' she shouted into the recorder. 'Jack, Jack are you there?'...

The red light flashed its signal on the answering machine.

*

At 8.05 am the police radio crackled into life.

'Proceed immediately to Beech Cottage on Hill Road. Suspicious death. Woman's body discovered by cleaner. Possible suicide. No husband around. Forensics on their way.'

The police came upon the fatal crash scene. A jagged branch had pierced the windscreen and impaled Jack through the heart like the pointing finger of an avenging accuser.
    On entering the house later, the red light on the answering machine beckoned them to listen to the message.

Caroline was apprehended at the airport.

*

The Visitor

It was a still, late autumn day and I'd taken the chance to cut down some overgrown shrubs before the daylight faded. On my way to the compost bin with an armful of branches, a slight sound made me glance round, startled. A young girl was standing behind me. The sight of her made me drop my bundle with shock. She looked about fifteen but was wearing old fashioned clothes and her eyes were wide with fear.

'H...How did you get into my back garden?' I exclaimed. 'The gate is bolted.'

'I dinna ken,' she gasped. 'Where am I? Whit place is this?'

'What do you mean, where are you, this is my private garden,' I retorted. 'Did you come through the house?' I made a step towards her, at which point, she folded to the ground in a faint.

Hurriedly pulling off my gardening gloves I knelt down at her side.

Her skin was very pale against her thick, wavy brown hair which spread out over the grass. She was wearing a long-sleeved blouse under a woollen pinafore with another cream linen pinafore on top. Her legs were clad with brown button boots.

Was she acting in a play or as a film extra? I stroked her forehead as she gave a little moan and opened her eyes.

Immediately, her fear returned and she tried to stand up. 'Who are ye?'

'I'm Sue,' I answered, helping her to her feet. 'But more to the point, who are *you* and what are you doing here?

'I … d…dinnae ken how I got here. I wis on my way to the Mill… I felt a bit dizzy an' then … an' then found masel' here. Where is this?'

'You are in Pittenweem. Where do you live?'

'Pittenweem? I've niver heard of that.' She shook her head. 'I bide in Hawick. Is it near here?' Her lip started to tremble.

At that, I took in a deep breath. 'I think you should come inside and have a drink of water.' I led her gently by the arm towards the back door.

I eased her into a chair at the kitchen table and fetched a glass of water. She held it with shaking hands and took a large gulp. Her eyes were wide as she looked all around the room.

'Whit's that, please?' she asked, pointing to the cooker.

'Why, that's my electric oven. I've just had a new touch control induction hob installed. Does your mum have gas?'

'I … I dinna ken whit ye mean.'

'You know – for cooking and baking.'

'We use the fire … and there are wee ovens on each side,' she ventured.

'Mm. You told me earlier that you lived in Hawick and were on your way to the Mill. What were you going there for?'

'I work there.'

'You *work* there!' I exclaimed, 'But you look too young to be working anywhere, never mind in a mill.'

She lowered her eyes and I could see tears brimming over.

'Oh, I'm so sorry, I didn't mean to upset you. Here's a tissue to wipe your face.'

The girl looked in wonder at the paper tissue as though she'd never seen one before. 'Tissue,' she mumbled and gently wiped away her tears. Swallowing hard, she looked up at me. 'My Dad died last year an' my mither took me and my sister Mary oot o' school. We had tae gan tae work in the Mill.' She gave a shrug. 'We didnae hae enough money. I hiv anither sister, Nellie. She's younger.'

I stared, uncomprehending. 'I don't understand. The mills are nearly all closed now in the Borders, and children certainly don't work in them. What age are you?'

'I'm nearly fourteen,' came the reply with an indignant toss of her hair. 'Lots o' us hiv tae gan oot tae work. It's nae shame.'

'Forgive me, I didn't mean to imply that It was. It is just that - what you are telling me died out early last century. By the way, you haven't told me your name.'

'It's Annie.'

'Annie what?'

'Grossert.'

Something that I couldn't quite grasp, stirred at the back of my mind.

'Can I just get this straight?' I cleared my throat, took a deep breath and looked into her eyes. 'Your name is Annie Grossert and you live in Hawick. You are thirteen years old and are working in a mill. You have no idea how you came here – just arrived in my garden out of the blue.'

The girl nodded, dropped her head and burst into tears afresh. 'It's true, Missus … Sue. I dinnae ken whit has happened.'

'Well. I'm as flabbergasted as you. I think we could both do with a cup of tea.'

As I went about filling the electric kettle, Annie stared in amazement. I laid two mugs on the table and took the milk carton from the fridge. I lifted out the sugar bowl from the cupboard and as I glanced in her direction, she was sitting open-mouthed. The kettle signalled that it had reached boiling point with a loud click. I popped a teabag into each mug and filled up with the water. 'Here's a teaspoon if you want to add sugar or stir in your milk. You can put your teabag on this saucer,' I added, laying plates down as well. 'We'll have a biscuit too. Chocolate digestives or gingernuts?' I placed the opened biscuit tin in front of her. 'Help yourself.'

Annie closely followed what I was doing and lifted her teabag out of her mug with a spoon and placed it beside mine on the saucer. I offered to pour some milk from the carton and she nodded. Using her spoon, she copied me and stirred her tea. 'Just pop that on the table top,' I indicated. 'It wipes easily.' She tentatively laid down her spoon and looked at the biscuits.

'Please have one. I'm going to,' I said, reaching for a chocolate one.

Annie picked up the same and smiled shyly as she took a nibble.

'They're my favourites,' I ventured.

'I … I've never had yin o' these afore.'

'Oh. What kind do you like then?'

'Well … we dinnae usually hae biscuits.' She continued taking small bites. 'But Mum bakes shortbread at the New Year. I like that. She's a grand baker – maks lovely fruit cake an' scones.' Her eyes clouded, 'But since Dad died, there hasnae been money for makin' cakes.'

We sat in silence for a few moments sipping our tea.

'My husband will be back from the golf club soon. Maybe he will know how to sort all this out.'

Annie immediately stiffened. 'Oh, I dinnae want to be in trouble.'

'You're not in any trouble,' I patted her hand, trying to be reassuring but not feeling that Ian would be any more help than I in this weird situation. 'Here, have another biscuit and try to relax.'

I sat hoping to think of something to ask which might shed light on the matter.

'Em … the clothes you are wearing are quite different from mine, as you can see,' I said and pointed to her pinafores and my tee shirt and jeans. She just nodded and hugged her mug. I had a sudden idea. 'What year is it just now? Do you know?'

'Of course. It's nineteen hundred and eleven.'

'Nineteen hundred and eleven?' I spluttered. I didn't know whether or not to appraise her of the truth and sat for some moments rubbing my thumb along the rim of my mug. 'Annie,' I finally decided, 'I have to tell you that this is two thousand and twenty one.'

'What! How can it be? 'She jumped up knocking over her chair. 'How can I be in the future?'

'I don't know, dear, I don't know. I'm as puzzled as you,' I replaced the chair and eased her down on it again. 'Try not to-

'Hi Sue, I'm home,' called Ian from the hallway. The door banged and he could be heard walking towards the kitchen.'

'In here, Ian,' I answered. 'We have a visitor.'

Ian entered and smiled to the newcomer who was visibly shaking. 'Hello young lady. I don't believe we've met. I'm Ian, Sue's husband.' He stuck out his hand. 'I see you must be going to a Halloween do.'

'Ian, this is Annie Grossert. She comes from Hawick and,' I swallowed, 'I know you're going to find this hard to believe, but … but she's come from the year nineteen eleven. I er… found her in the garden a short while ago.'

'Oh, come on. You're pulling my leg.' He looked from my tense face to the white face of the young girl, and sensed that this was not a joke. 'Nineteen eleven? The year nineteen hundred and eleven?'

I nodded. Ian looked stunned and thumped down on one of the other chairs at the table. 'I'll get you a tea,' I muttered and busied myself preparing his mug.

'Tell me exactly what happened,' requested my husband so I related the events while Annie sat, fingers twisting her pinafore, eyes huge in her pale face.

'Well,' said Ian when I'd finished, 'I'm not sure who to turn to.' He got up and walked around the kitchen. 'Should we phone the police, or perhaps a doctor?' He was standing behind Annie at this point and tapping his finger against his temple.

'No, no! No' the polis. I hivnae din onything wrang.' She burst into tears afresh and I handed her the tissue box. 'I wis goin' tae the mill and felt dizzy.' She sobbed and looked at us pleadingly. 'I dinnae ken how I got here an' … an' I'm frightened. I jist want tae gan hame … tae my mither an' my twae sisters. Oh, they'll be that worrit if I dinnae gan hame.' Then she had another thought and gave a gasp. 'The Mill! The foreman'll hae reportet that I hivnae turned up fir the late shift. I'll be sacked! We winnae hae enough money. Oh, no!' she wailed and grabbed a handful of tissues. Burying her face in them, she wept noisily, her shoulders shaking.

'Let's not do anything hasty,' I suggested to Ian. 'She can stay the night in the spare bedroom and we'll see what happens tomorrow.'

'Oh, I'm not sure about that! What if it's all a big scam and she's a plant here to… to rob us, or something,' he declared.

I gave him a scathing look. 'A plant! How did you come up with that one? She's thirteen for goodness sake and obviously in shock.'

He just shrugged. 'It's up to you, then. I don't know what to make of it all. I'll away up to get out of these golf togs.'

Annie was still sobbing. I touched her gently on the shoulder.

'I'm going to make some dinner. It's just cottage pie and some broccoli and peas but there'll be enough for us all. Would you like that?'

Annie turned her red, swollen face towards me and nodded.

'Come with me through to the sitting room and you can watch some television. That will be something new for you,' I added, wondering what she'd make of that.

She followed me into the next room and I pointed towards an armchair. She sat down very warily and stared around at the furniture and decor in amazement.

'I'm just going to switch on this machine,' and I picked up the remoted control.

Annie jumped when the picture appeared.

'It's all right.' I soothed. 'You'll enjoy this. You'll see lots of wonderful things. It's called television.'

I set it to a wildlife programme and sat down nearby for a few minutes. Watching Annie's wonderment, I felt quite humbled. I tried to imagine what it must be like to be seeing a television set for the first time.

'I'll just be in the kitchen getting the dinner ready.'

Annie nodded but didn't move her gaze from the screen. It was a delight to see her calmer and a smile was lingering around her lips at the sight of penguins waddling on the ice.

When Ian came back downstairs, he walked through the living room and came into the kitchen. 'She's glued to the television. It must be so exciting for her.' He gave a little giggle.

'Hm. So you do believe her then? '

He didn't answer. 'Where's the paper?'

I pointed to the counter. 'I'm just making an apple crumble. Poor thing, I don't think she has many treats. The veggies will be ready in ten minutes so don't disappear.'

`I'll sit next door and watch the telly too. I hope there aren't going to be any lions eating gazelles or there'll be more tears.' He nodded in Annie's direction. 'Once we've eaten and she's feeling better, maybe we could get more information from her. Get advice about what to do. She seems a nice kid. Reminds me a bit of our Carole.'

He disappeared with his newspaper.

When the meal was ready, I called them through to the kitchen table where Annie took her seat shyly beside Ian.

'There you are then, dear,' I said, laying a plate in front of her. Just eat what you'd like.'

She gave a smile of appreciation at the sight of the food and said, 'Thank you,' quietly.

We ate in a strained silence. All of us deep in thought.

After the dishes were cleared away into the dishwasher to Annie's great interest, Ian suggested that we had a cup of tea. 'We can all have a wee chat about what can be done to help you Annie.'

He bustled around getting paper and a pen.

I switched on the kettle and opened a cupboard for the mugs.

'Now then, young lady,' Ian looked towards Annie with a smile. What is your full name?

'Annie Grossert, Mister Ian,' came the reply.

'And your address?'

4 Moorshill Green, Hawick.

At that, there was a crash as a mug dropped from my hands and shattered on the tiled floor.

'What happened there, dear?' asked Ian with concern. 'You ok?'

'It's … it's all right. My hand was wet… the mug just slipped.'

I fetched the dustpan and brush and quickly swept up the broken china. My mind was racing. *I should have known by her name straight away. That address just clinched it. What am I going to do?*

Through a haze I heard Ian asking Annie for her date of birth, and reeling off a list of questions finishing with asking if she knew anyone with a telephone. *What good will that do! She's from 1911 for goodness sake!*

I took a deep breath, and tried to lighten the situation. 'Would you like to see around the house, Annie?'

She nodded her agreement so I led the way upstairs.

'Ye must be very rich to hae such a lovely big hoose.'

'Oh, it's quite ordinary really. Just a three-bedroomed semi, but it's in a nice, quiet housing estate and handy for all the amenities.'

Annie looked perplexed.

'Sorry dear. I forget that you don't understand modern talk, as it were. I mean that our house is called semi-detached. That means it is joined to the house next door through the wall. We live in an area where a lot of new houses were built together, so we have a good bus service, convenient shops and church nearby and a Health Centre where we can go if we need a doctor.'

'But you must be rich,' exclaimed Annie. 'Ye have lotsa rooms and an indoor privy. Ours is outside. It's freezin' when the weather's snell,' and she gave a little shiver.

'Well, I suppose that compared with conditions in 1911, we seem rich indeed. Have a look in here,' and I pushed open the bathroom door.

Annie gave a squeal of excitement as her hands flew to her face. 'Oh, my! Oh, my! I've never been in a real bath. My twa sisters and me a' hae tae tak turns in a tin bath in front o' the fire on a Saturday nicht.'

'Then you shall have a lovely bath all to yourself tonight, dear.' I pointed to the shower cabinet. 'Or, if you prefer, you could have a hot shower? There's the toilet and washbasin and I'll bring you some towels.'

Annie was speechless with pleasure.

'Come and I'll show you the bedrooms. This one is ours,' and I opened the door.

'Oh, it's jist beautiful. I love the colour,' exclaimed Annie.

'It's called duck egg blue. Very restful,' I added moving along the landing. 'Next door we use this bedroom as a study and it's also my sewing room.'

'Whit's that machine?' asked the girl, pointing to the computer and keyboard on our desk.

'Well, it is called a computer.' I thought for a moment. 'Let's leave that until tomorrow. Ok? This is your room here across the landing,' and I ushered her into our spare bedroom.

There were more gasps of delight at the double bed, the duvet, the dressing table and fitted wardrobes. 'This room is just used occasionally when our daughter Carole comes to stay with her husband and the grandchildren. We have to put an inflatable bed in the study for the wee ones then.'

Annie was looking a bit nonplussed and I realised she was puzzling over 'an inflatable bed.'

I laughed and said, 'Come on, back to the bathroom. I'll give you a nightdress and dressing gown. Here are some towels. There's shampoo and body lotion there. Just use anything you fancy.'

I ran the bath and poured in some fragrant bubble bath liquid then left the room to fetch night clothes.

Annie was standing hugging the towels and gazing at the hot water longingly when I returned.

'Right. Here is a nightie and dressing gown for you and a pair of cosy bed socks as I don't have spare slippers. Here's a new toothbrush and toothpaste as well. I'll get out of your way now and give you some privacy. Take as long as you like. Have a good soak and come down when you're ready.'

It was with some relief that I walked downstairs and flopped onto the sofa beside Ian.

'Well, what are we going to do about her?' he enquired.

'I don't know. I really don't know. She's having a soak in the bath at the moment and is so delighted with everything I've shown her.'

'I still can't believe that she's really travelled through time. It's like a science fiction movie.'

'Uh huh,' I agreed. *I wasn't yet ready to tell him about the revelation I'd had earlier. I couldn't quite get my head around it myself.*

'It's too dark now, but in the morning, I'm going to search around the back garden,' declared Ian.

'What do you think you might find?'

'I don't know really, but there might be some clue. If this is all true, then we must have a vortex, or star gate or wormhole or… or something, outside.'

I nodded. I couldn't come up with a better idea for Annie's mysterious appearance, and just sat staring ahead, my thoughts turning over.

It was over an hour later when Annie came shyly into the living room. She was wearing the night clothes I'd given her and had a towel wrapped around her head.

'Did you enjoy your bath then?' I asked with a smile.

'Oh, aye! I was fair taen on wi' the taps, an' I've never had perfumed bubbles afore. I smell fair braw. Thank you. I washed ma hair too. I hope that wis alright?'

'Of course it was.' I rose from the sofa. 'I'll just get you the hair dryer and a brush and your long locks will be dry in a jiffy. Have a seat.'

'Hair dryer? Jiffy?' queried Annie, but she sat down and waited patiently.

She was thrilled with the process of drying her hair. I showed her how to brush her wavy tresses while I worked my hair dryer. Her hair was soon gleaming and soft.

'There. You look good. Would you like to watch some more television?'

'Yes, please. You're bein' very kind to me.'

I put on the Disney channel and she settled down happily to watch it. I signalled to Ian, and we went through to the kitchen.

'Don't put on the News tonight, dear. It might be a bit too frightening for her,' I said in hushed tones.

Ian nodded. 'Yep. She doesn't know about outer space, computers, mobile phones, air travel etcetera, etcetera. I don't suppose she's seen many cars either. Oh, that'll be a surprise for her tomorrow, if we take her out.' He stood thinking for a moment. 'The supermarket,' he announced. 'That'll be a treat. Lots of foodstuffs she's never seen before. You could take her to M&S and get her something to wear. Or Top Shop or some of the young people's clothes shops. That would be a shock for her.'

'Your right. The womenfolk in her era always wore long skirts and dresses.'

He laughed. 'I wonder what she'd make of young people paying a fortune for ripped and faded jeans! I can't understand that one myself,' he chuckled. 'Talking of understanding, it's hard to make out her dialect sometimes, isn't it?'

'Yes, the Borders tongue can be tricky until you get tuned into it.' *I remember that from a childhood visit.*

'I'll make us all a hot chocolate and perhaps she'll want to go to bed early. She must be worn out with all the unfamiliarity and she's obviously missing her family,' I said quietly.

When we walked back into the living room with the mugs, Annie straightened up quickly.

'Oh, I think I wis aboot fallin' asleep then. It's so lovely an' warm.'

'Well, have this mug of hot chocolate and then you can go up to bed if you like. It's been quite a day for you. Well for all of us really,' I added.

'Thanks, Sue.' Annie took a sip of the milky drink. 'Mm, delicious. Thank you too … Ian. I'm not used to callin' adults by their first name.' She took another sip. 'Ye've both been amazin'. I jist wish I knew how this all happened … an' how I can get hame.'

Her face crumpled and the tears fell once more.

I went and put my arm around her shoulders. 'Drink up your hot chocolate and try to get some sleep. Things will look better in the morning.'

She wiped her eyes on her sleeve and replied, 'That's what Mum always says too. Things'll look better in the mornin'.' She gave us a weak smile.

Ian and I spent a restless night. I lay awake going over the events of the day. *Was I right about who I thought Annie was? How could she have travelled through time? Why had she come here? Was I supposed to do something with her? If so, what? What if she disappeared the way she came? Would she have any memory of us or would she go back without missing her shift at the Mill?* And so it went on all night with Ian obviously worrying about Annie too as he turned from side to side, in fitful sleep.

We both got up about 6 o'clock and went wearily downstairs. There was no sound from the guest bedroom. I filled the kettle and switched it on to make tea.

'Well, have you decided what we should do about Annie today then?' asked Ian, yawning and rubbing his eyes.

'Not really.'

'I suppose we should notify the police.'

'What if they don't believe us? We can hardly believe it ourselves!' I placed two mugs of tea on the table.

'I think we should phone the police and ask for someone to come to the house.'

I nodded. 'That's probably best. However, I'm terrified of the news getting out. Can you imagine what reporters would make of this? ... They'd say she was mad ... or we were mad... or worse, child molesters. People might think we'd kidnapped her ... brainwashed her or something, to say that she'd come through time, so that we'd get lots of money for our story.' I could feel tears pricking my eyes.

'Now, now don't get ahead of yourself. We will just tell the truth and it will all work out, you'll see.' He patted my hand and sipped his tea.

But I didn't feel his confidence.

It was after 7.30 before we heard sounds upstairs. I called up, 'Come down when you're ready Annie and I'll make you some breakfast.'

'Thank you, Sue,' came the answer.

Annie appeared in the kitchen a few minutes later, hair brushed and looking tidy.

'I hope I didnae oversleep. It's still quite dark ootside so I didnae ken whit time it wis.'

'That's no problem. It's not yet eight o'clock and there's no rush to go anywhere. Were you warm enough?'

'Oh, yes. That doovy thing was so cosy. At hame I hiv a cardigan and socks on in bed, as weel as a hot water bottle, loads o' covers, an' a sister!' she added with a laugh.

Her mirth however, changed straightaway at the memory of home, and her face became serious. 'Hiv ye decided whit to dae aboot me?' She looked from me to Ian.

'After breakfast, I'm going to give the police a call and we'll take it from there. Don't worry, you're not in any trouble. Perhaps they will be able to suggest someone we could contact for help,' answered Ian.

'Meanwhile, what would you like to eat for breakfast? What do you usually have?'

'Well, we sometimes hiv porridge and sometimes jist toast and margarine.'

'I could make porridge or perhaps you'd like some breakfast cereal? We just have Muesli or Bran Flakes I'm afraid.' I showed Annie the two packets. She looked at the pictures and read the description.

'They baith sound good,' she answered.

'Well then, why don't you have a mixture of the two?'

She nodded and looked on with obvious pleasure when I poured the cereals into a bowl, and poured milk on top. 'Would you like some sliced banana and a few blueberries too?'

'Yes, please, Sue.'

'It's a pleasure to see you so happy', commented Ian.

'Cup of tea? And how about some toast too?'

'Mmm, that wid be grand,' Annie mumbled through her spoonful. 'Thank you.'

After breakfast was cleared away, I fidgeted around the kitchen, wiping surfaces and putting off time. Ian was the same. 'I'll just pop out to the bin with this,' he said and disappeared outside. I knew he was using delaying tactics and didn't want to phone the Police. He wanted to look around the garden for clues as well.

I'd put on a washing earlier and the machine had finished so I unloaded the clothes.

'Could I go out to the garden too?' Annie asked me when she saw I was about to hang out washing.

'Of course. It's calm and mild again. I don't know if the clothes will dry, but at least they'll get an airing,' I said with a smile and we walked out into the back garden.

Annie handed me a sheet and I began to peg it up. Ian came over beside us. He mouthed to me, 'Nothing,' and shook his head. 'What a nice autumnal morning. Maybe we could all go for a walk to the woods later. Would you like that Annie?'

When there was no answer, I looked up from my basket and saw the shock on Ian's face.

'What is it?' But in an instant, I knew.

'She … she's gone. She was just standing there … and then before my eyes… I can hardly believe it … she just … faded away and disappeared.' Ian stood motionless.

I stumbled the few steps towards him and we stood, Ian's arm around my shoulder, staring at the place where we'd last seen Annie.

'Now we'll never know who she is, or was,' Ian murmured.

'I know.'

'What?'

'I know who she was.' He took my shoulders and turned me towards him. 'I …I couldn't say before. She would have asked me to tell her what I knew about her life. How could I tell her that she would live through two world wars; that she'd marry and have two sons? The older son would marry and have a girl and a boy – her grandchildren, but her younger son would die from a brain tumour out in India. She was very gifted in crafts and needlework. She would be widowed in later years and die at the age of 79.'

'How do you know all of this? Have you suddenly turned psychic?' gasped Ian.

'No. I vaguely recognised the name Grossert but it didn't ring any bells at first, but when she talked about her sisters, Mary and Nellie, and then told you her address in Hawick, I knew.

'Knew what?' urged Ian.

'That Annie was my grandmother.'

May Magic

'Well, did you wash your face in the morning dew like you planned?' asked my friend as she settled into a chair in the coffee shop. 'Are you more beautiful now?'

'Oh, it was disastrous,' I answered and sighed, placing our two cups of coffee on the table and dumping the tray on the floor at my side.

Leigh scrutinised my face and replied with a frown, 'Yep, still the same old ugly mug. It didn't work then?'

'I set the alarm for -

'Two paninis with roasted vegetables,' announced a waitress plonking the plates in front of us along with cutlery and napkins. 'Can I get you anything else?'

'No thank you,' we both replied at the same time.

'Enjoy,' she said, smiling, and left us.

'Do you know that this is a panina, not a panini?' asked Leigh, not waiting for an answer.' Panina is the singular and panini is plural in Italian. There is no such word as paninis.'

'Is that so? Someone ought to tell the restaurants then.'

'I heard it on Radio 2 yesterday.'

'Oh, well, it must be right then,' I replied. 'Anyway, to get back to my sorry tale, I set the alarm for five thirty and got up, not exactly bright, but with great intentions. I put on my fleecy dressing gown and decided I'd better tie my hair back so that it didn't get all wet and grassy. However, my elastic band pinged away somewhere when I tried to use it, so I just grabbed my shower cap and put that on. When I opened the front door, it was barely dawn and still quite misty. Perfect; there was a lot of dew covering the front lawn but rather than get my fluffy slippers wet, I pulled on Mum's tartan wellies that she uses for walking the dog. I didn't have my contacts in and there was no point in putting on my specs to rub dew all over my face.'

'What a picture you are creating,' said Leigh through a mouthful of food. 'I wish I'd seen you,' and she laughed.

'Oh, don't,' I said, groaning. I took a bite of my panini and munched for a moment. 'I had to kneel on the grass, so got my pyjama knees wet, and I was busy rubbing dew all over my face when this male voice said, ' Er, excuse me, can I help you? Are you looking for something?'

'Never!'

'Oh, yes! I nearly jumped out of my skin. When I looked in the direction of the voice, all I could see was a blurred face.'

Leigh was giggling helplessly.

'It wasn't funny. There I was in a short red fleecy dressing gown, turquoise pyjamas -'

'With wet knees!' interjected Leigh.

'Tartan wellies and a yellow shower cap with red hearts on it. *And*, my face all wet and shiny with bits of grass sticking to it! Dad had been out with the lawnmower the night before and the bin thing that collects the grass wasn't collecting properly.'

Leigh was laughing hysterically now and people at the other tables were looking over at us and smiling, wondering what the joke was.

'Oh, May,' she gasped, wiping her eyes, 'what happened next?'

'I can't remember exactly, but I think I muttered something about searching for a contact lens!'

'Oh, no, not that old chestnut!'

'Ooooh yes!'

'You sound like that nodding dog in the insurance adverts.'

'Thanks.'

'So, what happened next? Did you speak to the guy? Was he hot?'

'I...I think I just turned and ran indoors. I was so embarrassed. I've no idea what he looked like but I know *I* looked a mess.' I took a few sips of coffee. 'Honestly, as if I'd be out at half past five in the morning looking for a contact lens! He must have thought I was demented! He did have a nice voice though, and it was kind of him to offer to help.'

'Maybe he's gorgeous and is your Mr. Right,' suggested Leigh. 'You could get up at five thirty again tomorrow and catch him coming down the road. He was probably going to the station.'

'Well, I think I pretty well ruined any chance that there might have been with whoever he is.' I sighed. 'He'll be married anyway, knowing my luck.' I finished off my panini. 'I'd just like to meet a good man.'

'Oh, that's someone I don't want to fall for, a Mr. Good.'

'What do you mean?'

'Well, my first name is Fairleigh shortened to Leigh. Imagine me going through life called Fairleigh Good?'

It was my turn to laugh now. 'Or how about Fairleigh Low or Fairleigh Small?'

'Oh, very droll.' She opened her bag, 'Oops, I almost forgot May, sorry. Happy Birthday,' and she handed over a small package and card.

'Thank you so much'. I tore off the paper. 'They're really lovely,' I said, admiring pretty moonstone earrings. I ripped open the card. 'To a Special Friend,' I read. 'Aw, that's nice. Thanks again.'

'Are you doing anything special tonight?'

'Well, Mum has invited Gran and my sister and brother-in-law for tea, so that'll be nice.'

'Not very exciting though. Let's go out on Saturday and celebrate. We could try the new Italian in the High Street and maybe go on somewhere from there? Anyway, we better get back to work. I'll text you,' said Leigh with a smile as she pushed in her chair.

*

I was tired when I got home from work after being up before dawn, but showered and changed for my birthday tea. Everyone thought my morning exploit was hilarious when I told them as we ate our meal.

'Me and my friends all washed our faces in the morning dew on May Day when we were young,' said Mum, laughing at the memory. 'However, I don't recall anyone ever saying that they'd worn such a colourful assortment of clothes for the procedure. I also don't think it made one jot of difference to our complexions,' she added.

'I did exactly the same when I was young,' said Gran laughing 'We all hoped for some magic.'

The doorbell rang.

'I wonder who that can be?' said Dad not moving.

'Well, I guess I'll have to be the one to find out,' answered Mum, rising and giving him a shove on the shoulder when he didn't budge.

She came back into the room moments later and announced, ' There is a rather charming young man asking if he can see the young woman who had lost her contact lens this morning. I asked him to step into the hall.' She was grinning at me. 'Go on then, he's waiting.'

I was in shock. I could feel my face going bright red as I struggled to my feet and walked into the hallway, closing the door behind me. There stood a dream of a man. His eyes opened wide with a look of approval when he saw me.

'You can't be the girl who was crawling about on the lawn this morning?'

I nodded dumbly. ' 'Fraid so,' I managed to mumble. Why was my brain not connecting with my mouth? This gorgeous guy will think I'm witless.

'Well ... you look ... beautiful now.' He shuffled awkwardly.

We both stood there feeling a bit embarrassed. My stomach was doing cartwheels. He thinks I look beautiful!

'Er... why are you here?' I managed to ask.

'Oh, em, I work as an optician in town and thought perhaps I could bring you the kind of lens you need. I had to go in early yesterday to do some preparation work. Um, that's when I saw you, er … on the grass.'

'How kind of you to - '

The door opened and Mum stuck her head round.

'Would you like to join us, young man? We're having a birthday tea for May. You're too late for the meal but just in time for some cake.'

'Oh, em, I wouldn't want to intrude,' he answered graciously.

'It wouldn't be an intrusion. You're very welcome,' I insisted. 'I haven't asked you your name. I'm May.'

'And I'm Alan. Alan Day,' he answered with a warm smile for everyone as we entered the living room.

Alan Day. Day? May Day! Help! I was running ahead of myself a bit. Wait till Leigh hears this one. My heart was pounding and my hand shaking as I handed him the plate with a slice of birthday cake. Maybe there is some magic in these old traditions after all!

The Group

'I can smell incense!' Jen stopped. She made as if to turn back. 'I knew it would be all that mumbo-jumbo stuff.'

I held her arm. 'It's ok. Come on, let's get in. It's too cold to hang about.' I gently pushed her through the door into the corridor. I'd already assured her that she'd enjoy it. 'They're a nice crowd. Hang your coat up here.' I pointed to the pegs as I shrugged off my jacket.

Jen was glowering. 'I feel more uptight than ever now!'

'Come on,' and I opened the door into the small hall. Inside, the blinds were drawn. It was warm and there were candles arranged in the centre of the floor casting their soft light around. It took a moment for our eyes to become accustomed to the change.

'How nice to have a new person here today. Is this your friend that you were telling me about Anne?'

'Yes, this is Jen. Jen, meet Avril, our leader.

Jen's hand went out stiffly and she gave a nod of her head in acknowledgement.

'Please sit wherever you'd like,' Avril offered.

'We settled down side by side in the circle of chairs and I gave a small wave of greeting to the others I knew.

'I don't think I'll like this. It's too weird,' whispered Jen. 'It's like a coven.'

'What's weird about it? You've seen candles before, and the music is lovely.'

Avril spoke. 'I think we'll just get started now. Welcome to Jen today. I hope you enjoy the meditation and feel relaxed afterwards.'

Jen just put her head down.

Avril rang a little bell then asked us to settle ourselves comfortably and close our eyes. She led us through a slow relaxation process from feet to head.

I was aware that Jen was still fidgety.

Next, we were led gently through a meditation where we concentrated on our breath; just following it in and out, in and out. Beautiful instrumental music was playing quietly in the background.

I sensed that Jen had settled.

When it was time to come out of the meditation, Avril rang the little bell again and told us to open our eyes when we were ready and to let our gaze rest on the candles. We could have a stretch if we wanted.

I was pleased to hear a big sigh from Jen.

After a few minutes sitting in the peace, Avril asked if anyone wanted to share any thoughts. No-one offered – they just wanted to sit in the silence.

She turned towards Jen. 'How are you feeling Jen?'

'Well … actually, I'm feeling very relaxed thank you. I…I didn't think I would be able to meditate,' she looked around the group who were smiling. 'I thought you were supposed to sit cross-legged or maybe do chanting or something.'

'Oh, well we could do that next week then if you like,' said Avril with a wink to me.

'Oh, no, er … the way you do it is fine,' said Jen.

When we were putting our coats on to go, I smiled and nudged Jen, 'So you're coming next week to our coven then?'

'Yes, sorry Anne. You were right. I did enjoy it. I haven't been so relaxed for ages. Mmm. The warmth and darkness felt like a womb.'

'Oh, hark at you, all new-agey sounding.'

'Everyone was so nice and they are just normal, like us.'

'Glad you enjoyed it. I'll let you know when it's your turn to bring a goat for the sacrifice,' I said with a straight face.

Maggie Balfour

I wandered into the bedroom, towelling my hair as I walked and picked up my phone from the dressing table. I'd heard the familiar warble while coming out of the shower. A missed call from Anne had gone to voicemail. I quickly followed the automated directions and Anne's voice burst into the room.

'Jenny, Jenny… It's me! Help me! They're coming for me!'

There were muffled angry voices in the background then a loud bang and the sound of splintering wood followed by scuffling and shouting.

I heard Anne scream and scream … then nothing.

I stood motionless, staring numbly at the phone in my hand. Then flinging off my dressing gown, I jumped into the clothes I'd laid out, scraped a brush through my hair, grabbed the phone and with shaking hand, locked the door and ran from the house. If only I hadn't decided to take a shower in the afternoon!

I didn't stop running until I arrived down at the shore at Anne's house. Gasping for breath, I hammered on her door and pressing down on the latch, lurched straight into the small living room.

'Anne, Anne … Are you here?' I shouted as I ran from door to door. There was no answer.

While wondering what to do for the best, I noticed my friend's laptop open on the dining table and I scrolled up to read the following on the screen …

To whom it may concern,

My name is Anne Cameron. I have decided to write down an account of the events that have occurred recently in order to bring some understanding should anything happen to me. I've included conversations that I remember. Somehow, I have become entangled with the life of a young woman, condemned as a witch nearly four hundred years ago and have been experiencing first hand, many of the horrors she suffered.

Let me explain. I'd always longed for a house with a sea view. My late husband loved the countryside so I compromised and lived inland. However, Tom has been gone for four years now, so I decided to move to the coast and follow my dream. On reflection, I can see that the dream turned into a hideous nightmare, but how could I have known?

I can't believe how everything just fell into place. When I saw the cottage for sale in the fishing village, I fell in love with it straight away. As I walked through the doorway with the agent, I had a feeling of déjà vu. The house was originally built with others in the row in the 16th century, for fishermen and their families. One bedroom looked out to the River Forth over a small quiet beach area, and another looked over the terraced back garden. Feeling that it was just perfect, I rented the cottage.

Everything went smoothly at first and I loved my cosy home. I enjoyed sitting with a coffee, gazing out of the window at the ever-changing sea and sky. I joined local groups and soon made new friends. It was a pleasure to go walking on the windswept coastal path and trudge along the many beaches in the surrounding district. After a few months I was completely convinced that I'd made the right decision to move here. Then things started to change.

One Sunday morning last winter, I'd been busy in the kitchen preparing for a friend coming to lunch. The soup was made and I had a dish of lasagne ready to heat. I was in the process of setting the table when there was a loud rat-a-tat at the front door.

Puzzled, I hurried to open it and was immediately pulled out into the street by a woman wearing a long black coat and a straw bonnet. 'Hurry up, Maggie,' she hissed at me as she banged my door shut behind us. 'Ye ken the meenister winnae like it if we're late.'

She grabbed my arm and hurried me along the road. I couldn't speak. What was going on? Whoa! ... I couldn't believe what I was seeing. I was dressed in a long brown skirt and coat of some rough material and I too was wearing a bonnet. I had old but well-polished boots on my feet and was carrying a bible in my gloved hands. When I glanced around, I realised that my familiar scenery had gone. Where was the fish shed; come to that, where was the harbour wall and lighthouse and the fishing boats? There were two large dilapidated vessels lying at anchor near an old jetty piled with coils of rope, nets and broken fish boxes. Unfamiliar shops were shuttered; stalls and carts straggled along the foreshore. There was no sound except for the screaming of gulls and our hurried footsteps. The woman urged me quickly up one of the steep wynds where we joined other people making their way towards the church. As we walked through the gate into the churchyard, we were greeted by another woman.

'Mornin' Maggie; Mornin' Jean. Freezin' wind today,' she said as she nodded and smiled in our direction.

'Mornin' Jessie,' answered my companion, who I surmised must be Jean. I think I nodded dumbly in Jessie's direction and followed the others into the church. We slid into a pew at the back just before the doors were closed. The minister entered and climbed up steps to the pulpit, where he bent his head in prayer.

I don't remember the service that followed as I was numb with both fright and cold. What on earth had happened? Had I slipped through some portal into another time? That must be it. What year was this? I surreptitiously looked around at the packed congregation from under my bonnet. There were hardly any men; just some who were very elderly and a few youths. It was mainly women of all ages, most of them looking shabbily poor. I felt dazed and reacted mechanically as required when we stood to sing the psalms or bent to pray. One thing I do recall clearly was the minister. He was small with greying hair and a pinched face, but appeared large in stature when he controlled the proceedings with his angry voice and pointing finger. I remember how he shook with rage as he addressed the congregation, warning them that yet again, it had come to his attention that a witch was active in the village.

'I will find her ... and she will confess ... and be purified!' he spluttered. 'God is on my side, and He will be avenged.' His fist thudded down on the edge of the pulpit. 'Amen.'

He glared at everyone as his head moved slowly around, missing no-one. I looked down as his gaze fell on me, fearful of meeting his eyes.

'You're very quiet th' day,' Jean said, giving me a nudge as we walked from the church.

'I'm not feeling very well,' I answered, which was quite true by then.

'It's so freezin' cold in that church. What with that and all the talk of witches, I'm no' surprised you're feelin' ill,' she answered.

We walked on in silence until we came to my door.

'Bye then. See ye tomorrow. Hope you're feelin' better,' Jean said and gave me a cheery wave.

I nodded, then hesitated at the door. Summoning my courage, I pressed my thumb down on the brass door latch and pushed the door open. I can't tell you the relief I felt to find my own living room as I'd left it earlier. When I stepped inside, I was once more wearing my usual trousers and warm sweater and had slippers on my feet. When I looked at the clock, an hour and three quarters had passed and Jenny would be arriving at any moment.

I walked shakily through to the kitchen and switched on the oven, but my legs threatened to give way so I slumped into my armchair. That's where my friend found me when she arrived a few minutes later.

'Anne! Whatever's the matter?' Jenny asked. 'Your face is white. Are you feeling ill?'

I decided it was best not to say anything as I hadn't yet got my head around the situation.

'I just felt a little dizzy for a moment, that's all. I must have got up too quickly or something.'

'Well, you just sit still and I'll see to the lunch,' Jenny said, and busied herself.

Over the next few weeks, nothing untoward occurred and I was beginning to think I must have dreamt everything, when it all started again.

One afternoon, I suddenly found that my sitting room had been transported back in time and it was shabby and sparsely furnished. I was sitting talking with Jean as we huddled around the fireplace where some driftwood sparked from the salt as it smouldered.

'They've got another witch!' Jean whispered excitedly and hunched closer to me. 'I heard they've got her in the Tolbooth. They'll get a confession soon enough I reckon, once they start the prickin'.'

'Oh, the poor thing,' I answered.

Jean looked at me in surprise. 'Poor thing indeed! I wonder about you sometimes, Maggie. It wis witchcraft that's caused the fishin' tae fail an' the plague an' all. She's in league wi' the Devil!'

She pulled her shawl tightly around her shoulders and stared at me. 'I wonder sometimes if ye're no' a witch yoursel'; what wi' thon herbs ye grow an that cat ye keep.'

'Ye know I use the herbs tae add taste - goodness knows there's little enough food - an' for healin' potions.

Jean sniffed.

'An' ma cat! She's good company.'

'Well, maybe that's no' how the Council wid see it,' Jean retorted.

Without warning I found myself back in my comfortable, familiar sitting room, feeling shocked and bewildered. Was I in danger? Was this Jean likely to hand me over as a witch? I felt like I was going mad.

Not knowing what to do, this time I confided in my friend Jenny, who suggested, 'It sounds as though either you have lived in the cottage in a past life, or you have somehow tapped into the energy of Maggie who lived there. It must have been in the late 1600s or early 1700s.'

We decided to do some research, and after much reading and enquiries, discovered that there had been many 'witch' burnings carried out with the approval of the Church. The town council was paid handsomely for each witch who 'confessed' and was eradicated; the minister having his large share of the takings. Over the years, a series of hardships had left the town depleted of men. Many were lost in battle; others succumbed to the plague, then the fishing failed. Poverty, fear and superstition were rife.

I was lying comfortably in that half-awake state the next morning, when I was transported to a stinking, dark, stone building. I was Maggie again.

'Here is thy confession ready to sign,' my gaoler thrust a parchment at me. 'I'll read it out. *I, Margaret Balfour do admit to using witchcraft to cause harm. I have renounced my baptism and admit I am in league with Lucifer. My familiar lives with me working enchantments.*' He flapped the document in front of my face. 'Admit it and save yourself a lot of agony. You'll be burned anyway.'

I was filthy, cold, starving and in terrible pain. All my hair, including my body hair, had been roughly shaved off. I had been beaten intermittently for days, kept awake and left with no comfort but straw on a stone floor; but I refused to confess this untruth. I summoned enough strength to shake my head.

'Very well, take her upstairs to the prickers,' he ordered two rough-looking men.

I was dragged up stone stairs to the next level, thrown to the floor and chained to the wall by my wrists. The prickers had long, sharp needles which they proceeded to plunge into my legs every few minutes, working systematically from the ankles up to the calves. I screamed and screamed as the pain caused me to shudder in and out of consciousness. My blood spurted and spattered the straw-covered floor.

'Confess, witch,' hissed one assailant. 'We'll keep prickin' till we find the Devil's mark.'

'We ken ye have the Devil in yer blood. It needs to be boiled oot o' ye in a pyre,' growled the other.

Thankfully, I suddenly found myself back in my own bedroom. I was shaking and terrified by the ordeal I had to all intents and purposes just suffered. I kept checking with relief that my legs were unhurt. When I felt calm enough, I phoned Jenny, and we met at her house so I could relate the latest horrors.

'We must perform a ritual or blessing of some kind to lay this poor lost soul to rest,' Jenny declared. I'll phone a therapist friend and establish the appropriate words, and we'll do it tomorrow,' she assured me.

I know that something has to be done soon, so I'm going to stay with Jenny tonight, until we've performed whatever is necessary to release Maggie from my life. When I came home to pack my overnight bag, I decided to record the details of my experiences so far.

A short while ago, while I was sitting writing, I was again transported back to the Tolbooth. This time, I was in a dreadful emaciated state. My legs, arms and breasts, swollen and covered with crusted blood, were excruciatingly painful from continued pricking. I lay sobbing on the filthy floor, longing for death to take me. Someone opened the door and came towards me.

'Margaret Balfour, do ye confess that ye are a witch now?' a man's voice asked.

I could hardly form any speech. My parched, cracked lips tried to move. 'Yes,' I croaked. I would have confessed to anything to have release.

'Sign here,' he said thrusting a quill into my shaking hand which he guided over the parchment.

'You will be taken to the Priory, tied to a post with barrels of pitch and burned to death. As you have renounced your baptism, there will be no Christian burial. If your family has money, they may request to have you strangled prior to execution. That way they do not have to witness your agonies as your blood boils and the fat melts off your bones. Do you understand?'

I nodded with horror then watched as the hazy form of this official opened the door, leaving me in pitch blackness. *I have no family left!*

I am back at my table again. I must stop shaking. Time is running out! It seems that the 'witch' experiences are becoming more frequent. Am I going to experience Maggie's death-throws? I am absolutely terrified of what might be before me. I'll be leaving soon to go to Jenny's for the night, thank

WilliamSage@SOS@btinternet.com
Cameron.j@gmail.com.au
Dear Mr. Cameron,
Missing Person – Anne Cameron
As requested, I attach a copy of the document retrieved from your mother's computer. This will perhaps shed some light on her recent disappearance however unlikely it may seem. As you can see, it would appear that she was

interrupted while writing her account. The police are meanwhile continuing to conduct their enquiries and are questioning neighbours and friends of the above.

Jenny Connelly, a close friend, has confirmed that the events as described in the attached document related by your mother to her, are a true account.

It would seem that your mother, although apparently in good physical health, may have some mental health issues causing her to hallucinate and perhaps lose her memory. The police are circulating her description through the media nationwide, and expect to hear of her whereabouts soon.

I will keep you informed when we hear any news. Be assured that your mother's property has been secured and her personal belongings have been collected for safe-keeping. We await your further instructions.

Yours sincerely,

William Sage
Sage, Osborne and Semple Solicitors
South Street
St. Andrews, Fife.
Attch

Sorry Missus

'You take a turn on deck now Joe. Helen can go with you for some fresh air.' Chrissie settled herself on a folded rug on the hard wooden seat and pulled another travelling rug around her shoulders. 'I'll see if James will settle down for a sleep now.'

'Ok. C'mon love,' he beckoned to Helen. 'We'll be able to see the sunset over Ailsa Craig.'

Chrissie sighed and pushed her hair back from her face. 'I'm getting a bit of a headache. It must be the noise and the smells.' She nodded, indicating the stout mother opposite who was carefully shelling hard boiled eggs into a brown paper bag and handing them out to her brood.

Helen wrinkled her nose in disgust. 'I'm needing some fresh air myself away from the smell of beer.'

'Bye, Dad,' James murmured sleepily as he settled across his mother's lap.

Joe smiled and gave him a pat. 'Try and get some sleep yourself then,' he whispered to his wife. 'Bye for now.'

He turned as he stepped onto the stairway leading up to the deck and mouthed, 'Won't be long.'

Chrissie smiled and nodded.

She looked down at ten-year-old James already asleep. Pulling his coat over him, she tried to ease herself into a more comfortable position. The wooden seats were all they were allocated while travelling steerage. She must stay there keeping their places and looking after their bags. Pulling the travelling rug tighter around her shoulders, she closed her eyes trying to blot out the sight of other holidaymakers and workmen on their way to Dublin. The constant rumbling of the engines, the chatter and shouting all around and the smell of beer drifting up from the bar was distressing for Chrissie. Trying to shut out the noise and think about their holiday in Dublin, she imagined the boarding house, the parks and shops. This was the first time she'd been out of Scotland and how she wished they'd been able to afford a cabin.

'Whoa! Sorry Missus.'

Abruptly Chrissie's eyes flew open. She jerked her head away to avoid the offending rancid breath from a dishevelled, drunken man who was sprawled over the suitcases. He was bearded with straggly grey hair and his clothes were dirty and tattered.

Staggering to his feet he repeated, 'Sorry Missus,' and touching fingers to his forehead in salute, he lurched off to drag his way upstairs.

'He's been up and down to the bar all evening,' volunteered the man in the next seat. He shook his head. 'What a state to be in. Are you alright?'

'Yes, thank you.' She turned her attention to James who had stirred with the commotion. 'It's ok. Go back to sleep again.' His eyes closed.

I wish Joe and Helen would come back. They were going up to watch the sunset over Ailsa Craig, but it's getting dark.

Her headache was getting worse. She chewed her lip. People were making themselves comfortable with cushions and blankets. At least it seemed quieter now as passengers settled to rest.

Minutes later, urgent shouting could be heard from above deck. Everyone stirred and listened.

'They're shouting, man overboard,' called someone near the stairwell.

There was a tangible tension in the air. Then the silence was shattered by the sound of a claxon and the ship began to turn around. The engines were cut. The ferry heaved up and down.

'A flare's gone up!' yelled someone.

'What's happening?' asked a sleepy James. 'I think a man may have fallen overboard,' Chrissie whispered, trying to ignore her thudding heart. 'We'll just have to be patient and wait and see what happens.'

'Where's Dad?' James looked around. 'And Helen?' he persisted.

'They've sent out men in a dinghy now,' someone called. There was a large group of passengers craning to look out of the windows. 'It's too dark to see. We must be miles away from where the person went over. They'll never get the poor blighter now.'

'Your man hasn't come back dear,' said the stout woman.

I know that, Chrissie screamed in her head. Don't you think I know that!

'He - he'll be here s-soon,' she blurted. Her mouth was dry and sticking together.

The woman tilted her head to the side and smiled sympathetically. 'I hope so, dear. I hope so.' She hugged two of her offspring to her.

'What shall we do Mum?' asked James. Before Chrissie could answer, there was a commotion on the stairs and two crewmen hurried towards her. They directed Chrissie and James to grab their bags and follow them. One of the men picked up the two suitcases and they were hustled to the upper deck while passengers stepped back out of the way, whispering and pointing.

It must be Joe. It must be Joe. What are we going to do? Chrissie felt her knees buckle and one of the men grabbed her elbow.

'It's going to be alright, Missus. We're taking you to see the Captain.'

James began to whimper. 'Has something happened to Dad and Helen, Mum? Why are we going to the captain?'

'I – I don't know, pet.' *I do know. They must have drowned. Oh, God. Oh, my head. I can hardly see for the pain.*

They were ushered into a small office where a man with a white shirt and gold epaulets, was standing with a handful of papers talking to someone.

'Dad!' yelled James and rushed forward to hug him.

'It's ok Jimmy. It's ok.'

Through blurred eyes, Chrissie made out her husband and daughter standing by a desk.

She rushed to them and clutched Joe's arm, gasping, 'I thought it was you. I thought it was you

… overboard.' She turned to hug Helen who stood white and tight lipped.

Never one to show public affection, Joe patted her shoulder.

'Oh, we're fine. Sadly, we saw a man jump over the stern. We were too high up to do anything. I could only shout for help. He didn't try to swim. He even put his head under the water.'

'I needed your husband to make a statement,' said the captain. 'An elderly couple saw the incident too. We are going to give you a steward's cabin for the rest of the night. It will be a bit cramped for four, but will prevent you from being pestered.'

The captain indicated a chair for me.

'I'll bring some tea, Missus,' said a steward.

'Who was the man who jumped overboard?' Chrissie asked.

'We don't know his name unfortunately,' answered the captain. 'He was a foot passenger and we don't log those names. Apparently, he'd been drinking since he boarded.'

'Must have been building up Dutch courage,' said Joe putting his arms around Helen and James. 'Poor soul. He must have been in a terrible state to take his own life like that.'

Chrissie recalled the drunk man who'd fallen against their cases.

'Sorry Missus.'

She jumped.

The steward had returned with a tray of steaming mugs, milk, sugar and biscuits.

'Could I just get past to lay this on the desk for you?'

The captain leaned towards Joe. 'If you'd just sign and date this form here sir that will be all I need.'

Joe took the fountain pen and duly signed and wrote the date 10th July, 1961 and handed it back.

'Thank you. Well, I don't expect the body will be recovered, but if it is, it will have been washed up in New York'. He turned with a twinkle in his eye, but a serious expression and said, 'You'll need to go and identify it.'

Nosey Neighbour

'Yer always cleanin', James,' prattled Lizzie, dropping cigarette ash on the freshly washed hallway tiles.

James tried to ignore her, but as usual she persisted in passing on her gossip.

'That one above me had her fancy man visitin' last night again.' She drew on her cigarette. 'Her bloke'll be back at the weekend. Works in London. I'll let you know if I hear any arguments. Or anything else,' she added with a grin, giving him a wink and a nudge and dropping her stub into the bucket.

'I'm really not interested,' James replied through tight lips. 'Now I must get this dirty water emptied' and he entered his flat kicking the door closed behind him.

'That woman!' he muttered. She was always hanging around listening to and watching everyone's comings and goings. 'I wish she'd leave me alone.'

'Off on your dog walk then?' called Lizzie later that morning, pretending to polish her letterbox. 'I could set my watch by you. 10am and 7pm,' she laughed. Giving Micky a pat, she said, 'You've got him well trained, Micky. He's a well-behaved master. Very punctual.'

James nodded and hurried off with his dog before she captured him again. 'Well behaved master, indeed! That woman!'

He enjoyed having his routines. Keeping busy was the only way to cope with being on his own. He tried to keep the flat as Betty would have done and Micky was all the company he needed.

Next morning, Lizzie could hardly wait to break the news that the 'fancy man' had visited upstairs again, *and* stayed the night *and* was still there, but James didn't appear as usual to sweep and mop. When ten thirty came and went, she became anxious and knocked at his door and looked through the letterbox. There was no sign of James, just Micky barking madly and jumping at the door.

'Something's happened to him,' she said aloud, pondering. 'I know, we need someone with a ladder to reach in that small open window.'

She bustled upstairs and rang the doorbell of the house above hers. A man in overalls answered.

'Oh, can you help please?' she panted. 'I'm sure somethin's happened to the widowed gentleman downstairs. His dog's been barkin' for ages. Do you have a stepladder?'

'Sure thing. I've been doing some decorating for my sister. I'll be right down.'

James had fallen in the bathroom and split open his head. He was floating in and out of consciousness when he was aware of Micky barking, then voices, then the familiar smell of cigarettes as Lizzie leaned over him.

'You'll be fine, James. The ambulance is comin'. I'll keep Micky for you.'

'Thank God for nosey neighbours,' smiled James to himself.

Vikings

"That's my pal, Mike from Australia on Skype, Jan. I'll probably be a while as he'll want to know all about our new abode," Ted called from the dining room where he was sitting with his laptop.

"OK dear. I'm busy making soup for tomorrow's lunch anyway. Give him my regards." Jan carried on chopping vegetables and glanced apprehensively out of the window while she rinsed her hands at the sink. *There they are again,* she thought. *I'm definitely seeing them, but no-one else seems to.*

She closed her eyes and opened them again and looked down the sloping headland towards the sea. *Yes, they were still there.* "Ted!" she called, then remembered he'd be ensconced on his computer. He wouldn't believe her anyway. She'd told a friend and *she* hadn't seen anything either.

"Oh, we're really loving it here," Ted was telling Mike. "It's been well worth the year of renovations to be able to live in our very own castle. Well, not exactly a castle, it's been a watch tower or a keep or something, in the past, but it's just a fine size for us. It's square, so it was easier to convert into reasonable living space than a circular building would have been. We just have one large bedroom with ensuite bathroom upstairs, a large living room..." he prattled on, telling his friend all the details of his 'castle'.

Jan was starting to feel the panic rising. She could see the wild-looking men at the foot of their hill.

"The walls are three feet thick and we have the original heavy wooden door," Ted was saying, "That should keep out any marauding hordes!" he laughed. "I feel a bit like a laird. Jan sends her best wishes. Yes, she's fine, but she's bothering me a bit," he let his voice drop, "She insists that she is seeing Vikings, of all things, either in longboats down at the shore, or climbing up the hill towards us. She's convinced that every time she sees them, they get nearer. Of course, there's nothing there. I can't see anything, but I just try to reassure her and calm her down." He gave a conspiratorial laugh. "It must be her age. Yeah, the change. And she's always had a fanciful imagination. Remember she went on that creative writing course a few years back and wrote all those daft stories? It's probably some kind of reaction to all the stress of the building work and then the move, even though she insists she's fine and enjoying the peace and quiet."

"Ted!" shrieked Jan from the kitchen. "They're coming up the hill fast! They have axes and swords! Ted! Ted!"

"I'll need to go Mike, she's at it again. Sorry. I'll call you next week. I better go and calm her down."'

He signed off and wandered through to the kitchen. "Now, now what's all this?"' he asked kindly, then stopped abruptly as he saw the terror on Jan's face.

"The Vikings - they're here!" she screamed.

Ted's placating mutterings were drowned out by an insistent thundering on the heavy front door, followed by the sound of wood splintering and breaking glass as a huge axe smashed through the kitchen window…

Travelling Light

'Mum, you can't possibly take just that tiny case for a whole week! You're going to the sun in the south of France remember? You'll need lots of changes of clothes, plus all your makeup - although I don't suppose you bother much about that at your age - and lots of suntan lotion, sun hat, sandals, handbags oh, and what about swimwear?'

'I have everything I require,' I answered calmly, trying to ease my daughter towards the bedroom door, but she was not to be budged.

'What *do* you wear to the pool or beach?' Claire asked pointedly. 'I hope it's not still that same old swimsuit you had when you used to take me to the swimming baths when I was little,' she laughed. 'You are too old for a bikini of course, and anyway you wouldn't want anyone to see your midriff bulge,' she added dismissively, 'so I expect you have a firm tummy-shaping swimsuit, or is it one of those tankini things?' she prattled on.

'I've told you. I have all that I need,' I replied, trying not to show my irritation.

'Now, just think about it,' she hurried on, holding up a hand. 'You'll need your shorts or crops and a t-shirt for going to breakfast, then you'll need your beach stuff - oh, and take a sarong, that's great for covering a multitude of sins, ' she added looking pointedly at my tummy. 'Then you'll need to dress for dinner. Sundresses and perhaps a long floaty skirt with a few different tops, and accessories to match every ...'

'That's enough!' I interrupted. 'I'm just taking a few things that I can interchange, and plan to travel light this year. I don't need my daughter to tell me what to wear for goodness' sake.'

'Oh, well then, all right. I bet Dad's case will be bigger than yours at this rate.' Claire retorted. 'Karen, come up here and try to talk some sense into our mother,' yelled my eldest to her sibling.

'What's all the fuss about?' Karen answered, hurrying upstairs and breezing into the bedroom.

'Tell Mum that she can't possibly take all she needs for a week's holiday in that tiny suitcase.'

'Good grief, Mum, I take more than that as cabin baggage! Let's see what you've got.' Karen made to unzip the case but I put my hand firmly on it.

'Look you two. I'm really grateful to you both for coming home to look after the cats and the house for the week, but I refuse to be instructed about what to take on holiday. I *have* travelled before, believe it or not.'

'Oh, well, suit yourself,' Karen said huffily as she stomped out of the room.

'Thank goodness we're not going with them,' said Claire in a stage whisper, 'we'd be embarrassed to be seen with two tramps.'

'I heard that, madam, and I can assure you that your Dad and I will *not* be taken for tramps.'

*

'Are you looking forward to it then, darling?' smiled Alan as we boarded the plane.

'Oh, yes. I can't believe how hard it was to keep the girls from discovering. It's good that the two families can have a break together at our house, and the grandkids will enjoy the change, but I really couldn't bring myself to tell them the truth.'

'Well, not long to go now and we'll be sunning ourselves by the sea,' Alan said sighing happily.'

*

Alan turned the hired car into the palm fringed driveway past the sign, boldly proclaiming – Peacecove Naturist Village, and drove through the security gates.

The apartment was beautiful, with bougainvillea and oleanders in bloom around the patio.

'Let's quickly get settled, then we'll go and explore, and find a place to sunbathe,' I suggested.

'I'm so glad we came upon that beach last year, and found out how freeing it was,' said Alan, squeezing my hand.

'I love the way there is no embarrassment. Everyone is equal. You could be chatting to a judge or a cleaner and it makes no difference.'

Half an hour later, we were ready. 'Will I do then?' I asked mischievously,

'Absolutely' grinned Alan. 'You are wearing my favourite suit! I'll carry the towels.'

We went off hand in hand laughing. *'Whatever would Claire and Karen make of this,'* I thought, *'wearing nothing but my earrings, sunglasses and lipstick.'*

*

Too Little Too Late

The church clock struck eight, so those villagers who were awake knew without checking that it was six. Rosa was sipping her coffee and turning over the events of yesterday in her mind.

The previous morning, Rosa and her father were locked in an argument.

'I don't care that you've come all the way from Greece. That was *your* choice. I am NOT going back with you and I am marrying Andrew tomorrow at two o'clock whether you like it or not. I'm old enough to make my own decisions about *my* life.'

'But Rosa, why on earth do you want to marry this man when you could have a nice Greek boy? It's what your mother would have wanted,' he wheedled.

'Don't try that emotional blackmail. It won't wear with me,' Rosa retorted. My mother worked herself to her death keeping the home and that taverna going while you sat around on your fat backside smoking and drinking and playing cards with your lazy friends, never lifting a finger to help.'

'A man has a right to some pleasures.'

'Pleasures! What pleasures did we women ever have! My sister, Lena, had the same hard life, doing laundry, cleaning, cooking, working in the bar until all hours, and she looks like an old woman now! She never had the opportunity to marry. You saw to that, keeping her tied to the house and then the taverna. Working for a pittance!'

'Ah, but she met a nice Greek boy who came in to the bar, and is going to marry him soon. She is going to live at his home and work in his souvenir shop.'

'First I've heard of it! Well, good luck to her, is all I can say. She deserves to have a better life. I hope her new husband treats her better than her father has.'

'Rosa, Rosa, I will have no-one. Who will run the taverna when Lena goes?'

'So! That's why you want me back. To be your skivvy again. Well, it won't be happening!

She paced the floor for a moment, then turned and pointed a finger as she carried on with her rant. 'I'm glad I got out when I did and started a new life away from you. My Andrew has a bakery and we *both* work hard. We'll have a chain of shops some day! You'll see!'

'Please think about this, Rosa. I need your help now. I'm an old man,' he pleaded. 'The taverna will be yours one day if only you marry a nice Greek boy and...'

'Enough! I'm staying here in Scotland. No more of your conditions! Please go. I've nothing more to say to you.' She opened the front door and waited for him to leave.

'Your mother would turn in her grave if she could hear you.'

He shuffled out.

'My mother wouldn't be *in* her grave if it wasn't for you. Good ... bye' and she closed the door firmly, giving it an extra push. She leaned against it and let the tears roll down her cheeks. 'Oh, Mama, Mama. I wish you could be with me here today,' she whispered.

The church clock struck two. Moments later, there was a rat-a-tat-tat at the door. She managed to switch on a smile and put the unpleasant incident to the back of her mind when her good friend Beth arrived in a flurry, to help with her hair and makeup.

'Let's have a glass of fizz, Beth.'

'Oh, that will be lovely. How are you feeling? Excited?' Then she noticed her friend's reddened face. 'What's up? Have you been crying?'

Rosa nodded. 'Just a touch of wedding nerves, I guess … and I'm missing my mum.'

'Just you think of Andrew and how proud he's going to be when he sees how gorgeous you look in that beautiful dress,' Beth said, pointing to the bedroom door which stood ajar. A white gown could be seen on a hanger on the wardrobe door. 'Come on, let me work my magic on you.' And they both giggled.

The clock struck four and the wedding proceeded smoothly. Rosa was relieved that her father had not disrupted the ceremony and was nowhere to be seen. As the happy couple emerged into the sunshine, friends and customers showered them with dried breadcrumbs.

'What an appropriate sort of confetti for us,' laughed Andrew, 'and it's environmentally friendly.'

Rosa's father Spiros, had been doing a lot of thinking and had decided to make peace with his younger daughter. He stood hidden quietly to the side while some photographs were taken, then as the couple moved towards their bridal car, he stepped forward. Catching Rosa's eye, he mouthed, 'I'm sorry.'

She nodded to him then turned away with Andrew.

Spiros spent the rest of the day down by the sea. He sat on a bench for a while watching the steady ebb and flow of the tide, thinking about his life and what Rosa had said. Had he been the cause of his wife's early demise? Surely not. Women were meant to look after the home, cook and clean and serve, weren't they? The world seemed to be changing and maybe he was out of step with it. He forgot to eat. He just wandered around, an elderly foreign man with a stick, dressed in a light-coloured suit and a hat. Not a common sight in these parts.

After some hours, he decided to return to the church to talk with his God. Finding it hard to climb up the steep hill from the shore, he realised he should have had a meal and hot drink. By the time he reached the church gates, he felt very weak and struggled to open the catch on the wrought iron gates. After slowly making his way along the path, he came to the heavy wooden door and gave it a push. It was locked. Anger grew inside and he cried out, 'So you have shut me out too!'

Tears sprang to his eyes as he balled his fist against the door, and while banging on it in vain, a crushing pain slammed into his chest. The last thing he heard were the chirruping sparrows enjoying the remains of their wedding feast as the clock struck eight.

. . .

Next morning, the church officer pulled up at the gates to the churchyard, jumped out of the car and was lifting boxes of cakes from the back seat as the church clock chimed eleven.

'Stupid clock!' she grumbled to herself. 'When are they going to sort it? '

Struggling to turn the handle of the wrought iron gates while balancing the boxes, her shoulder bag and the ring of church keys, she staggered through the gate which clanged behind her in the wind.

She crunched along the gravel path and jumped, as what appeared to be a hat, suddenly careered round the side of the building and went bouncing off among the gravestones.

'Good grief! Where did that come from?' she exclaimed, then turning the corner, she dropped her armful in shock at the sight before her.

There, sprawled across the few steps leading up to the church door, was the body of a man. His face was contorted and his eyes were wide open. He was obviously dead.

Shaking, Ruth fumbled around in her bag for her phone and punched in 999.

'Th…there's a dead man … ly…lying on St. John's Church steps,' she stammered and tried to listen carefully to the questions that followed.

'Ruth Johnston. I'm the Church Officer. No, no-one else is here. No, I haven't touched the body. Yes. Yes, I'll wait here.'

Shoving her phone into her cardigan pocket, Ruth picked up the spoiled cakes which had tumbled on to the ground, tutting to herself as she dropped them back in the boxes. She walked a little closer to the man's body. He was wearing a light linen suit, the kind you might wear in a warm country, like Italy, she decided.

'He looks a bit Italian, come to think of it,' she said aloud, taking in his dark hair and tanned skin.

A siren heralded the arrival of a police car followed by a white police van. A man and a police woman jumped out of the car and walked briskly towards Ruth.

'D.I Cameron, and this is WPC Jameson,' announced the tall young man indicating the police woman at his side while flashing his warrant card. 'What are you doing here at the church at 9 o'clock in the morning?'

'I was on my way to open up and start setting out the tables in the hall. We have tea and cakes after the service today. We always do this in the summer. It's kind of a way to welcome any holidaymakers who come to the church.' She glanced down at the boxes at her feet. 'However, we won't be having these cakes. I dropped them,' she stated with a sigh.

'Yes, well …there will be no service here today,' announced the Inspector. 'This is a crime scene and will be out of bounds until we establish the cause of death.'

There was a buzz and the policewoman answered her phone. 'Forensics are on their way, sir.'

Cameron nodded. 'Do you know the man lying there?' he asked Ruth and jerked his head towards the body. As he spoke, a tent-like affair was being erected around the doorway.

Ruth shook her head.

He asked more questions which she answered.

'Had she noticed anyone else near the church? What exact time had she arrived? Did she have the minister's phone number? Could she think of anything else that might be relevant?'

Ruth suddenly remembered about the hat. 'A hat blew round the corner as I arrived. It must have been his. It sort of goes with his kind of clothes. It flew off away over there.' She pointed towards the graveyard. 'I'll show you.'

As the group moved off towards the gravestones, sparrows took advantage of the moment to clear up the cake crumbs.

. . .

Sunday's Child

The Child who is born on the Sabbath Day is Bonny and Blithe and Good and Gay

My parents could have chosen to call me Bonny, or Blithe, but no, they decided to call me Gay. At the time of my birth, gay meant happy and playful. Nowadays of course, it has quite different connotations. Thankfully, throughout my school days, there was no problem but now each time I have to say my name, people look at me oddly when I answer, Gay. A word which could bring up all sorts of difficulties with political correctness. I was talking about it with my elder sister yesterday.

'Not at all,' my sister Grace – obviously a Tuesday child – declared. 'They'll just look at you and know by your age. Lots of girls born in the 1940s and 50s were called Gay.'

'Oh, gee thanks! That makes me feel a lot better. I don't think!'

'I think it's a lovely name,' she went on. 'Short and sweet. And it won't get shortened - or lengthened,' she added. I'm always getting called Gracey, which I dislike. I used to wonder what Mum and Dad were thinking when they decided to give me the middle names of each grandmother'

I smiled as she got on her high horse.

'Grace Alicia Marguerite Fotheringham. What a mouthful, and it takes ages to fill in a form! Your married name of Black gives you a nice short name at least.'

'Yes, I was spared the middle names, but *you* sound like an actress, or author or some aristocratic Lady.'

'Hah, that'll be the day. However, I do think perhaps I got some of Granny and Grandma's good qualities,' Grace said thoughtfully, pursing her lips.

Gay Black sounds so boring.' I gave a little shrug and sighed.

'Not at all. I think it sounds very business-like and important.' Grace picked up my phone which had been lying on the table between us. 'And now, over to Gay Black, our political correspondent in Westminster,' she mimicked with her pretend mike.

'Oh, I don't think that name would go down well in politics,' and I gave a wry laugh at the thought. 'Maybe foreign correspondent would be more suitable.'

'At least your surname is ok. Remember how we used to wonder what our last names might be when we married?'

'How could I forget Gordon,' I replied. 'Thankfully, I haven't had to go through life called Gay Gordon!'

At that, Grace jumped up and pulled me to my feet, stood at my side and yanked my right arm up to my shoulder so I could hold her right hand. Then she grabbed my left hand in hers and marched me across the floor. 'Dah dah da-ra-da-da-de' she belted out to the tune of *Scotland the*

Brave and we attempted to dance the Gay Gordons round the living room.

As we fell into armchairs, gasping and laughing, I panted, 'That was more like the Giggling Galumphers than the Gay Gordons, and your name is *Grace*?'

'Well, I'm not as slim and agile as I used to be, but I can still enjoy a good ceilidh.' After a few moments, Grace caught her breath and smiled. 'The other surname you dreaded was Abandon. Now that would have been something – Gay Abandon!'

'Help!' I shrieked. 'That would have been too much to bear. However, I suppose there was always a chance that I could have become Mrs. Gay Gordon, but I've never heard of Abandon as a surname.'

'Put on the kettle and make me a cuppa then, now that you're feeling a bit better,' Grace ordered.

A few minutes later, we were sipping tea and munching our biscuits, when Grace stopped what she was doing and just sat still looking at me.

'What? What is it?

'Well, I was just thinking that em … lots of people believe that er… before we come into this life, that is, before we are born, er… we actually choose our parents and where we'll live. Not only that, we impress on them what name we should have.'

Looking a bit red-faced, Grace busied herself eating her biscuit and studying her mug of tea.

I stared at her. 'I've never heard you mention anything like this before.' There was a slightly uncomfortable silence. 'It sounds a bit weird and New Agey. What do *you* think about it?'

Grace shifted around a bit, then looked me straight in the eye. 'Well, I have to say that it sounds like it could be true. To coin a phrase - it resonates with me.'

'What would be the point in choosing your parents and where you live?'

'Well, from what I understand, we are here on Earth to have experiences and to learn from them. If there was something in particular that we needed to learn, we chose, before we came in, the circumstances and people who would present us with these experiences throughout our life.'

We sat quietly for a few minutes while I digested this information. 'Where did you get this stuff from?

'Oh, lots of reading, lots of discussion and I've been on a few spiritual-type workshops,' Grace replied. 'I er... haven't mentioned it before because I didn't know how you would take it.'

'Mm.hm.'

She leaned closer to me. 'Think about this. Ask yourself what you have learned from your parents. Our parents. Some people are taught honesty, kindness or how to be independent, for example.'

I nodded slowly.

'Others may have chosen a very difficult experience with illness or disability, or even hunger or abuse.'

'Why on earth would anyone choose these?' I snapped, throwing up my eyes.

'Well, perhaps to draw attention to a situation that needs to be addressed, maybe at family level or even on a world scale. Like rape, murder or disease… or maybe it's so that you can learn to forgive, or to love.'

'I've never heard you talk like this before, Sis.' I rose and walked over to the window. 'You sound as though you are speaking … like, from your heart.'

'That's because I am,' Grace answered quietly.

I turned around. 'I … I'll have to take some time to think about all this. Do you have a book or something I could read?'

'Yes, I'll pop back tomorrow and bring you some that I've found helpful.

. . . .

Next day, when Grace returned with a few books, I told her I'd hardly slept, turning over in my head all that she'd said.

'I've tried to come up with some reasons why I'd choose the name Gay,' I ventured as she dropped the books onto the kitchen table. 'Mum always said I'd been a very happy and contented child.'

'Yes, you were,' agreed my sister. She pulled a chair out and sat down.

'That could be one reason I'd chosen the name. So that I'd be a happy person and that would make it easy for people to love me.'

'Yep. Go on.'

'As gay has now come to mean homosexual, and I'm heterosexual, er… it makes me feel awkward, or annoyed or… or angry to have to explain that it's just my given name. It is especially strange to young people who only know one meaning for the word.'

'Yes, I can understand that.'

'I think … perhaps … I must try not to get angry or confrontational about this and rise above any feelings of annoyance and become a happy person again.'

'Wow, you've really been thinking this through seriously. I'm impressed,' Grace was grinning.

'Well, I'm happy about that anyway,' and I laughed back.

'By taking responsibility for choosing your name, you can't blame Mum and Dad or anyone else now. You are not a victim. How does that make you feel?'

'Hm. Strangely, I feel lighter.' I smiled. 'And happy and gay.'

. . . .

. . .

The Laundry

No-one ever really knew what went on at that laundry.

I'd stuffed down the memories over the years, but today, on my return from work, they came flooding back.

'So, what did you do at school today then?' I asked my 7year old, Julie, as I gave her a hug.

'We learned a song from long ago when ladies wore long dresses and had maids,' she said excitedly jumping up and down. 'Shall I sing it to you, Da?'

'Of course. I'll sit here and be your audience.'

I sat on the settee and waited for her to start.

' *'Twas on a Monday morning, when I beheld my darling,*
She looked so neat and charming in every high degree.
She looked so neat and nimble-o, a-washing of her linen-o
Dashing away with the smoothing iron,
Dashing away with the smoothing iron,'

My insides contracted. I forced my face into a smile as Julie sang in her sweet voice and swung her arm backwards and forwards as though ironing.

'*Dashing away with the smoothing Iron, she stole my heart away.*

There's a verse for every day of the week, and we'll learn the Tuesday one tomorrow.'

'That's great, sweetheart,' I said, keeping the smile fixed. 'Have you sung it to Ma?

Yes. She thought it was good and said you would like to hear it too.' Off she skipped.

I let out my breath slowly.

Perhaps now it would be appropriate to find time to write down all that can be remembered. Contacting the people close to me will be easy enough, but will they want to be involved? I'll start the process tomorrow and see.

. . . .

I have written the following account after speaking with the friends and family concerned.

Robbie

I went back in my mind to that happy day a few weeks into my new summer job …

'Bye son,' called my Da, 'don't be falling for any of those pretty laundresses,' he quipped. 'Remember you're going back to university after the summer.' He waved and walked off to the bus stop.

'Robbie, here, don't forget your sandwiches.' My mother shoved my haversack over my shoulder. 'Hurry up. You don't want to be late.'

'Thanks Ma. See you tonight.'

I walked to the laundry wondering if that sweet girl would be at the door again. The building was set back from the road behind a high wall. It was part of a convent run by nuns, but apart from my interview with the Mother Superior, I'd never had anything to do with them. Stopping at the lock up, I opened up the door and backed out the laundry van. I took a moment to write the mileage in the log book then closed the doors, clicked the padlock and drove the van to a side door. A stern woman in a grey shift dress was waiting.

'Help me with the baskets,' she ordered and I hurried to help her drag the heavy wicker loads of clean laundry which we heaved into the van. 'They're for the hospital. These are the parcels for the boarding houses as usual,' she pointed to a pile on the step, then picked up two parcels tied with string. 'And there are only two packages for the big houses today.' She shoved the latter into my arms.' The addresses are on them. They'll be billed at the end of the month.'

She turned away and slammed the door shut.

I shrugged at her lack of civility and looked down at the two heavy brown paper parcels in my hands. The addresses were on my way to the hospital, so I decided to go there first.

The 'big houses on the hill' as they were known, were grand mansions. Many are now divided up into flats, but in those days, most were owned by doctors and lawyers and the like. I soon arrived at the first address which I hadn't been to before. As there was a long, tree-lined driveway leading to the house, I decided to take the van up. The gravel drive divided and one part went to a side door and the other curved around the front where a large car was parked, then circled back upon itself.

I pulled up at the side door, thinking that would be expected, and knocked on the door. A woman appeared.

'Hello er, this is your Magdalene Laundry delivery, Mrs. O'Neill,' I said, offering the parcel.

'Thank you', the woman said, taking it. 'I'm not the lady of the house, I'm the housekeeper, Mrs. Dunn. You can collect again on Friday morning, 8.30.' Dismissing me with a smile and a nod, she turned away and closed the door.

As I moved towards the van, I heard raised voices coming from the front door.

'No, no, Daddy. Don't send me away,' came shrieks from a young lady. 'Please, please!'

'You are a disgrace to this family!' came the angry shouts from a man.

I stepped forward and peeped around the corner. I saw a young girl being pulled by the arm towards the car, presumably by her furious father.

"You are no longer any daughter of mine. Do you hear!' He shook her by the arm. 'You will never set foot in this house again! We'll leave the nuns to deal with you ... and your bastard!'

As he dragged her, struggling and sobbing towards the back seat, I caught the sideview of her silhouette and the tell-tale bump.

'Mummy, Mummy! Please, please,' she called, but her mother didn't appear.

The car doors were slammed and I ducked back as the car sped away with a spray of gravel.

Feeling very uneasy, I waited for a few moments, then backed the van from the side door. As I drove past the front of the building, I saw a woman holding a handkerchief to her face at the bay window.

I couldn't get the incident out of my mind as I made my way to the second delivery at the big houses. All day, my thoughts were churning as I went about my work. Usually, my mind was on sport and girls, but this apparent rejection worried me.

When I got home, I decided to tell my parents about the girl.

'Sure 'n' it's best to leave well alone, son,' my father said. 'It's none of your business. You don't know the whole story.'

'But Da, the girl was distraught. She was going to have a baby and she only looked about sixteen. How could her da have treated her so bad?"

My mother, who'd been very quiet, said, 'I've heard rumours from time to time that the unmarried mothers are looked after by the nuns until they've had their babies. They work in the laundry to pay for their keep. This girl that you saw will no doubt be cared for until after her baby is born, then she'll be able to go home.'

'But Ma, her Da said she was never to darken his door again! She wasn't his daughter anymore!'

'Hush Robbie. Put it out of your head. It was just his anger talking. As your Da says, it's none of your business and don't be asking questions at the laundry, it may cost you your job.'

The matter was closed and Ma set about serving the evening meal. I was directed to call the family to the table and given a warning look which suggested that I wasn't to mention the subject again.

As I sat at the table, I looked around at our happy family. I was aged twenty and the fifth of seven children. Two of my older sisters and a brother were married, leaving two older brothers and a young sister still at home. I could never imagine my Da throwing any of my sisters out of the house, no matter what they'd done. He just doted on his girls and though not one for an outward show of affection, we all knew that we were safe and loved. I couldn't get that girl at the big house out of my mind. I felt for her.

. . .

Amy

I sat trembling in the back of the car. My father didn't speak as he drove. Tears coursed down my cheeks and I wiped my face with the hem of my blouse. It was a short journey to the place I was being taken to, but I didn't like the look of the building when we arrived. Daddy opened the car door and indicated that I get out. Taking my arm, he marched me up to the carved, wooden front door.

'Stand still,' he ordered. He pulled the bell cord. We heard footsteps approaching and the heavy door was unlocked and dragged open. A nun clothed in black looked enquiringly at us.

'I spoke with your Mother Superior earlier in the week. I'm Mr. O'Neill and this is the girl Amy that

I mentioned. I arranged that she would be admitted to your institution. My wife and I want no further communication with her or her forthcoming child.' He pushed me forward.

The nun opened the door wider. 'Come in my dear,' she smiled. 'Thank you, Mr. O'Neill. We will take over from here. Goodbye.'

Daddy turned away without another word and I entered into Hell.

The nun said, 'Follow me,' and walked briskly along a corridor into a clinic. There stood two other nuns wearing white aprons, looking more like nurses.

'Take off all your clothes,' one of them ordered and the three nuns stared at my body as I slowly took off everything, my face burning with shame as I looked down at the floor. My clothes were shoved into a bag and I never saw them again.

'Now stand still, while I cut your hair,' one demanded.

I gasped with horror as the nun grabbed a handful of my long, auburn hair and hacked it off with shears. She continued removing the rest of my hair until it all lay puddled at my feet. I let out a wail and lifted my hands to my head to feel the results of this devilish handiwork, but they were slapped down.

'This is no place for vanity! You will atone for your sins by humbling yourself and working hard for the Lord.'

I was handed knickers and a shapeless, grey cotton shift which I hastily pulled over my head to cover my nakedness.

'Here are clogs for you,' A pair of worn, wooden clogs were dropped near my feet. I slipped them on. They were too big.

'They are too…' 'Shut up!' a nun interrupted. 'Do not speak to anyone and only answer to a nun. You will address us as Sister. From now on, you will be known as Ruth. You must forget your former identity.'

I was ushered, shuffling, along many corridors until we came to a large room filled with steam and noise. There were six huge tubs which women of assorted ages were stirring with big wooden paddles. Further along, I saw women rinsing sheets in great sinks before passing them through a mangle. Through the steam, I could just make out rows of women standing ironing. Some of these workers were pregnant.

'You can start with the washing,' a nun said, handing me a rubber apron and giving me a prod forward to the nearest vat of soapy laundry. 'Move it around with this wooden stick and if you see any stains, use the soap and scrubbing board. I'll be back later.'

'I took the proffered stick and found a place next to two other girls and started moving towels around in the hot water like them. We prodded and pummelled and I watched as they lifted out a towel onto the side of the vat, if it showed a stain. This was then rubbed with a large soap bar on a scrubbing board balanced on the side. The water was hot and my hands were soon red and raw with the heat and scrubbing. Everyone kept their heads down and no-one spoke.

My mind was racing. How could I endure this work? It seemed as though hours had passed. When could I get something to eat? I'd had no breakfast.

The nun who had given me the instructions returned. 'So, Ruth, I see you are fitting in well here. Hard work never killed anyone.'

I don't know about that, I thought.

Much later, my stomach was growling loudly with hunger. The girl positioned next to me glanced over.

'Food soon,' she hissed, and gave me a quick smile.

I gave her a nod of appreciation and we kept our heads down and worked on.

A hand bell was rung somewhere. I saw a nun motion to the women at the first vat to stop and move out to another room. They returned soon after and resumed their chores. The nun jerked her head to us indicating that we were to go with her. I followed the others into a large dining hall. We queued and were presented with a bowl of watery soup with some chopped vegetables floating in it, and a chunk of hard bread. There were jugs of water and tumblers on the long table where we sat. The nun held up a hand and everyone bowed their heads. She said a prayer of gratitude for the food, then we all joined in with the Amen.

I was very hungry but this feeling disappeared at the first taste of soup. It was ghastly, with no seasoning. I poured myself some water and drank it down greedily. I poured a second tumblerful and looked around at the others in case this wasn't allowed, but no-one noticed as they had their heads down eating. I tried to chew some of the bread as I knew I needed the sustenance, but I just couldn't swallow. Tears trickled down my cheeks as I thought of Mrs. Dunn's delicious cooking. How was I going to survive here? Within minutes, a nun appeared at our table and everyone stood up. I followed the others as they gathered up their bowls, spoons and tumblers and we handed them over to other women behind the counter.

We filed into toilet cubicles which were ancient, but thankfully clean. We were shouted at to hurry up, and returned to our positions around the vats in the washing room while the next group of women were being called in for their lunch. The girl beside me gave me a wink, but no words were spoken.

The afternoon passed quickly and I soon got into the routine of pummelling laundry and heaving the towels into the next vat where they were rinsed by another group. We had to keep tipping out the vat of dirty water and refilling it from the boiler. My arms and back were aching and my feet swollen and wet with splashes. I'd no idea what the time was, when a bell was rung. It transpired that we were to finish the task we were on and empty out the dirty water into a drain, and that was our day's duty finished. A nun came to inspect our work space.

'You, Ruth. Mop the floor dry. You're sloshing around here.' She pointed to where a mop and bucket stood and dismissed the others.

Watched over by the nun, I did my best to mop and squeeze out the water from puddles on the floor, then emptied the bucket.

'Pathetic girl! I'll make sure you learn to do it more thoroughly! Hang up your apron,' she snapped, pointing to pegs and then to the doorway, indicating that I was to go. 'I'll see you tomorrow' she snarled.

I hurried through the door into a corridor and followed it to a stairway. Not knowing where to go, and with no-one around to ask, I clumped up the stairs, struggling to keep on my clogs. There were many closed doors and through one of them came screams, followed by a voice shouting,' Shut up girl! What a fuss to make.'

I shuffled past the door and ducked into an alcove when I heard more prolonged screaming, then the sound of footsteps coming up the stairs and of someone entering the room where the cries were coming from. I could hear a woman sobbing then she wailed, 'No, no! Don't take it, please, please.'

The door opened and I leaned as far into the wall as I could, as two nuns swept past me carrying a small bundle. They were in a hurry and preoccupied with their task. I heard one say, 'Is it dead?'

'No, not yet, but it won't take long,' the other said. 'We'll let it have some fresh air,' and she laughed.

They disappeared around a corner and I stood trembling in horror against the wall.

Was that a baby they were talking about? Were they going to kill it? I waited until the sound of footsteps disappeared and there was only the sobbing to be heard coming from the room they'd vacated. I didn't dare to go in, but slowly made my way further along the corridor, hoping to find some of the other women. One of the doors had a KITCHEN sign on it. Moving very quietly, I turned the handle, pushed the door open and a cold draught struck my face. My attention was taken up by the scene before me. A tall sash window was pushed up and a tiny, naked baby was lying on the sill. I gasped and my hands flew to my mouth. Hurrying clumsily towards the child, I didn't hear the feet behind me.

Next second, I felt blinding pain as something slammed into the back of my head.

I came to with a buzzing in my head and a nun towering over me. I was lying on the floor.

'So, we have a nosey one here do we?' she exclaimed, giving me a kick in the side.

I yelped in pain. 'I was looking … for the others,' I managed to gasp out.

'Well, you won't find anyone here. They are having dinner. *You* won't be joining them tonight though. Come with me and I'll find a suitable place for a sinner like you!'

She yanked me to my feet, pulling me so that my clogs fell off, and dragged me along to a room which she unlocked with a key hanging with others around her waist.

'Get in there, girl and repent for your sins. We don't put up with interfering busybodies here.'

'B..,but I was just trying to find where to go for f...food,' I stammered. I'm new here and I …

'Shut up!' she bawled, 'Let this be a lesson to you!'

The door slammed, the key turned in the lock and I was left in the dark.

Gradually my eyes grew accustomed to my surroundings. From a glimmer beneath the door, I could make out that I was in a small windowless room. A pot lay near me, which I suppose was for my toilet needs, but no furniture. Nothing else.

I collapsed on to the bare floor and cried and cried. Sobs racked my body until I thought I might die. *How had I come to this?* I thought of my beautiful home; my pink bedroom with its soft furnishings and fresh bedlinen. *How could my parents send me to this appalling place?* Soaked with tears and weak from hunger and exhaustion I lay inert on the hard floor. *Oh Danny, my love. Rescue me from this hell. Please, please!* My poor baby growing inside me was kicking in agreement.

Robbie

I could not get the girl from the big house out of my mind. Every day when I called at the laundry, I looked around as much as I dared, but there was nothing to be seen from the outside. I did notice that the windows at the back were all barred. Over the weeks, it was not always the same woman who handed out the laundry for delivery in the mornings. I wondered if perhaps I might be able to ask some questions, but so far, no-one had looked approachable.

Today, when I drove into the yard, the sweet girl I'd seen once before, was waiting to hand over the baskets and parcels. I smiled to her as I jumped from the van and she gave a small nod of acknowledgement then put her head down.

'Morning. Is this all for me?'

'Yes,' she said in a whisper.

Just at that, a long scream came from somewhere above. The girl shuddered.

'What was that?' I exclaimed.

'It's one of the girls in labour,' she said with her back to the door. 'I'm not supposed to speak to anyone, so don't let it look as though we're talking.'

I helped wrestle the heavy laundry basket into the van with her help. 'Why can't you talk to anyone?'

'I don't know. It's just one of the rules. The nuns are always watching us and if we don't do things right, we get a beating or put in a cell in the dark for punishment.'

'What?' I stood open-mouthed.

'Sh. I need to go. See you again,' she whispered, and ran off into the wash house.

Another scream startled me back to my work.

I sat in the van in a layby for a few minutes before doing the deliveries, trying to get my head around what had just transpired. *Were the nuns really beating the laundry girls and locking them up in the dark? That girl certainly seemed genuinely anxious. What happened to the babies? Were there children in that building too?*

'I must ask that girl about the O'Neill girl tomorrow, if I see her. Maybe she knows her.'

Next morning, when I drove up to the laundry door, the same laundress was waiting with a huge basket. I felt a little flutter in my stomach. I smiled to her as I walked over and she put her head down, but looked up at me under her eyelashes. A nun appeared in the doorway, obviously checking up on behaviour.

'Do you know Amy O'Neill?' I whispered as we hauled a basket together.

'I'm not sure. We're given different names when we come here,' she said without looking at me.

'You boy! Get that basket loaded into the van. The parcels for delivery are on the step. Agatha, come inside and get on with the packing.' The nun stood glaring as I struggled to lift the basket into the back of the van. I picked up the parcels and jumping into the driver's seat, moved off as quickly as I could.

Well, that wasn't friendly. However, I now knew that girl was known as Agatha. Becoming aware of a sharp pain on the inside of my arm I realised that I'd given myself a deep scratch from a broken piece of cane on the wicker basket. It was starting to bleed profusely. I stopped the van and wrapped my handkerchief around my forearm, hearing Ma's voice in my head, repeating, *'Do you have a clean hankie?'* every day before I left for work. I smiled to myself.

I set off on my deliveries. The first one was to the O'Neill residence. As I pulled up at the side door, Mrs. Dunn was just coming in from the garden with some vegetables.

'Morning Mrs. Dunn,' I called.

'Oh, good morning son. Sorry I don't know your name?'

'It's Robbie.' I smiled and went to hand over the heavy parcel of linen. 'Shall I carry this into the kitchen for you? You have your hands full.'

'That would be very kind thanks. Oh, what have you done to your arm? You're bleeding!'

'I just caught it on a rough bit on the basket. It'll be alright,' I said as I followed her inside and laid the laundry parcel in a space on the scrubbed wooden table.

'Hmm. Best let me have a look at it,' said the woman, putting on her glasses. 'I'll just take off this hankie and … oh, yes. that needs cleaning and a dressing. Sit down and I'll just wash my hands.' She busied around and brought out a first aid box from the kitchen press.

She seemed very kind, and cleaned and bandaged my forearm, chatting amiably.

'Stay and have a cup of tea with me, if you have the time?' she added.

'Well, I think I could manage ten minutes.' I sat back happily.

Mrs. Dunn made a pot of tea and produced a slab of fruitcake which she placed in front of me. 'I'll just fetch the sugar and milk. Eat up that cake. Young men are always hungry, 'she laughed.

I didn't need telling twice and polished off the delicious cake in minutes. The tea was very welcome as it seemed a long time since breakfast.

The housekeeper sipped at her cup and sighed. 'It's good to have a young person in the house again. It's so quiet here now. Mr. O'Neill is abroad with work and … and there used to be the daughter, Amy, here too … but she's away now,' she added, lifting the teapot and offering to top up my cup. She changed the subject. 'Have you been working at this job for a while? It must be quite heavy work. Do you live locally? Oh, there's the rain on.'

She seemed agitated and didn't wait for my answers.

I leaned forward. 'Mrs. Dunn, you mentioned a daughter, Amy, a few moments ago. One week when I came here for the first time, I er … I saw a young girl being taken away by her father. I often think of her. Was that Amy?'

Realising I may have overstepped the mark, I sat back, half-expecting to be asked to leave. However, Mrs. Dunn just looked at me in amazement.

'Oh, you saw her then.' Her hand rummaged in her apron pocket for her handkerchief. 'Mr. O'Neill was distraught when his wife broke the news.' She dabbed at her eyes. 'We all were. Oh, the shame of it. Poor girl.'

'But why did he send her away?' I asked.

'He couldn't bear the thought of a b… er … illegitimate child in the family.' She sat deep in thought for a minute. Cradling her cup, she sighed, 'She'll be so homesick in that convent. I miss her as though she was my own girl.' Appearing to feel that she had said too much, she stood up and put her cup in the sink.

'Mrs. Dunn, I work at the Magdalene Laundry, as you know. Maybe I could find out how she is

... but I hardly go inside at all. Just to lift in the heavier bags.'

'Mrs. Dunn,' a woman's voice was heard calling. 'I've prepared the menu for tomorrow night for the Owens coming.' Her high heels tip-tapped towards the kitchen.

'It's Mrs. O'Neill,' the housekeeper whispered and turned towards the door as the woman entered.

'Oh!' she stopped abruptly when she saw me.

I jumped to my feet and bowed a nod to her.

'This is Robbie, a delivery lad,' Mrs. Dunn explained. 'He'd cut his arm so I bandaged it for him, and we had a cup of tea. I hope that was alright Mrs. O'Neill?'

'Of course. I hope it feels better now,' she said, looking towards my arm. 'Where do you work, Robbie?'

'At the Magdalene Laundry,' Ma'am.

Her face blanched. 'Oh. I'll speak with you later, Mrs. Dunn,' she said and turning, left the room in a hurry.

'I think I better go,' I whispered. 'Thank you for the bandage and the cuppa.'

I left straight away and Mrs. Dunn hurried out behind me.' You forgot to take the bag of sheets for the laundry.' She handed me a cotton bag containing the sheets. 'I'll see you when you bring that back'

I nodded.

'Will you try to find out how Amy is?' she asked, twisting her apron.

I looked at her sad face. 'I'll try, but I can't promise anything.'

Ruth

'I know that weeks have passed, but I've no idea how many. I don't even know if it's day or night! I feel dizzy with hunger and exhaustion all of the time. The nuns are so cruel. I've been washing and rinsing and starching and folding. They had me scrubbing the floor in the long corridor on my hands and knees, then I had to clean and disinfect all the toilets and sinks! Oh, Danny, I can't believe things are so bad. What will happen to our baby? I so wish that you were here to talk to, and to take me away to anywhere but here.'

I was in the solitary cell once more and talking aloud to the darkness. A key ground in the lock. 'Who are you talking to? You know talking isn't allowed!'

Lying on the floor, I felt the swish of the nun's long robe as she towered over me.

'I was praying,' I replied, hoping to pacify her.

'Huh, you'll need a lot of prayers to atone for *your* sin,' she spat the words at me. 'Come to your breakfast. You have plenty of work waiting.'

I eased myself up and limped along behind her. The same large clogs having been returned to me, continued to make life even more miserable.

Breakfast was bread and dripping. I'd learned to eat everything like the other women did. It was the only way to get a little energy. Imagining that I was eating a poached egg on hot buttery toast or munching a bacon roll helped me to swallow the slimy lard. We were also allowed a mug of tea which was welcome. As usual, we filed into the toilets then walked towards the laundry room.

At the entrance, unusually, a nun stood with an armful of starched, white aprons and mob caps. 'Today, you are going to have a special treat. The local newspaper is sending a photographer to take photos of our superior laundry and you women at work. You will each put on an apron and a cap. Keep them clean,' she warned as we each took the items in amazement. Ruth, Agatha and Keziah, you are on the ironing and steam press today.'

I pulled the cap over my head like the others, to conceal my tufts of hair, tied on my apron and went to be shown how to press sheets and pillowcases and table linen, then how to iron shirts, blouses, underwear and nightwear for our customers. There was also a pile of grey cotton uniform shifts to be ironed.

However, before we began, the photographer and a reporter arrived. Nuns appeared around us, smiling and pretending to be helpful. 'Smile and look happy at your work,' hissed the nun nearest to us. The public need to see how good we are to you all.'

The resentment in the room was palpable.

I lifted my lips up at the corners and held the pose as the photographer moved slowly around the washroom with his camera flashing towards each group.

An elderly nun I'd never seen before entered. She was smiling beatifically and looking the picture of kindness as she drifted around the small knots of women working at their tubs, but was in fact dripping poisonous words from her parted lips as she passed. 'Look happy or you'll never smile again,' I overheard.

The reporter moved forward to accompany her as she made her way towards the ironing area. 'Mother Superior, is there anything you'd particularly like me to write about your laundry and the workers?'

'Well, as you can see, we have some young unmarried mothers working here.' She flicked a hand in my direction. 'We take care of them and their babies, while they work for their keep and atone for their sin.' She indicated another girl, well advanced in pregnancy, who was struggling to keep her smile going. 'Bring in a stool for this poor girl, Sister Rose. She shouldn't be standing in her condition.'

If it hadn't been for the noise from the steam machines, the man would have heard audible gasps following that remark.

The photography session was over after a few more minutes, the Mother Superior and newspaper personnel departed and the nuns descended like black bats, demanding the return of the aprons and mob caps. These were then thrown into a tub with the order to get on with washing them. The stool was whipped away from the heavily pregnant girl, who staggered against the vat. 'Ha, you didn't think you were going to keep that, did you?' sneered a nun.

I could see that the girl was livid but I wasn't prepared for what happened next. Despite her size, she lunged forward, screaming crazily. Wrenching the stool from the nun's grasp, she began laying into her with it. 'You evil bugger,' she shrieked. 'I've never had a kind word ... or a decent meal ... only beatings ... like this!' and she demonstrated visibly.

I was standing with my hands clasped to my mouth as nuns appeared from all directions. Everyone froze as the poor girl was hauled away. The nun on the floor was helped to her feet and assisted, hobbling from the room.

Mother Superior appeared. 'Get back to your work!' She whirled around, glaring. 'Anyone who thinks they can treat their benefactors in this way, **Will Be Broken**, as God is my judge.' She swept from the room as a flurry of activity broke out.

The three of us who'd been allocated to ironing, were each given a pile of bedding and table linen, for individual customers. I used a pressing machine to work my way through sheets for a local hotel, followed by tablecloths, pillowcases and napkins. Agatha and Keziah stood at ironing boards amid clouds of steam, pressing linen for the private house customers.

We continued like this all day, with only our short food break. Each bundle, once pressed had to be folded and carried through to the room where it was packaged for delivery.

Agatha was dumping a large quantity of linen on the table as I entered with one of my hotel bundles.

'That's me finished with the big houses' laundry,' she whispered as we stood together. 'They have some lovely stuff.' She wiped her brow and gave me a brief smile as she hurried away.

The big houses! I wondered if Mummy's linen was here. *Of course! She always sent the sheets and tablecloths to be laundered. Mrs. Dunn took care of our personal clothes and any delicate items.*

When I returned to the ironing station, I risked whispering to Agatha. 'Where would I get a pen or pencil to write a note?

She thought for a moment as I pretended to sort some linen. 'They need pens to write the addresses on the parcels in the packing room.' Steam hissed as she smoothed over a grey uniform.

'Thank you,' I mouthed, and returned to my duties.

Next time that I took a bundle through for packing, I looked around and spotted pens lying beside the ledger. No-one was looking, so I secreted one in my palm and went over to the table to dump my ironing. As luck would have it, I could read my own home address on a parcel nearby. Making sure nobody was paying attention, I tore a small edge off the brown paper package, scribbled HELP ME. Amy. and pushed it under a flap secured beneath the string. Feeling a flutter of excitement, I replaced the pen and went back into the ironing bay, giving Agatha a hidden, thumbs-up sign as I passed her.

Robbie

I'd been wondering how to contact the O'Neill girl. There had always been a nun overseeing the laundry bags being delivered and collected. Perhaps Mrs. Dunn could help me with a plan.

'Good morning, Mrs. D, 'I called, as I jumped down from the van. 'Lovely weather today.'

'Yes, it is. The blue skies lift the spirits, to be sure.'

I handed over the parcel and the housekeeper took it with a nod. 'Oh, I've got your handkerchief. You left it last week. Coming in for a cuppa?'

'That would be good, thanks.'

I sat down at the table and Mrs. Dunn had the kettle boiled and cups and saucers ready in no time. 'Here's your hankie. All washed and ironed,' she said, handing it over.

'Great,' I said, putting it into my pocket.' My arm is a lot better now, thanks to you, *Nurse* Dunn.' I showed her my healed arm.

'Well, I'm pleased to see that,' she said, laughing as she laid down a plate of digestive biscuits.

We sat amiably, drinking our tea and nibbling biscuits.

'I hope you don't mind me asking you this, Mrs. Dunn, but … do you happen to know who the baby's father is? I…I was just thinking that there's maybe something that he could do.'

She looked me straight in the eye, as though deciding whether or not to trust me.

'As a matter of fact, I do know. His name is Daniel Murphy, and a very nice, hard-working young man, he is to be sure, but Mr. O'Neill wouldn't allow Amy to have any more to do with him, once she was in the family way.'

'Does Daniel know about the baby?'

'Oh, yes – and he offered to marry Amy, but Mr. O'Neill would have none of it. He's a hard man … How could he hold his head up in the community and the church with a daughter who'd got pregnant before marriage!? That's what he said. Oh! I shouldn't be speaking about him to you like this.' She buried her nose in her cup.

'It's alright, Mrs. Dunn. I won't be gossiping. Do you know Daniel's address? Perhaps between us we can come up with some kind of plan. I'm concerned about Amy's welfare after hearing a snippet from one of the girls.'

I went on to tell her how the young laundress had seemed afraid of the nuns and said that they weren't allowed to talk or they'd get a beating. I didn't mention about hearing screams.

The housekeeper was visibly shocked. 'Oh, no! I thought the girls would be worked hard but didn't think they'd be beaten! Oh, Mrs. O'Neill would be beside herself if she knew that her darling daughter was being mistreated. She never wanted Amy to be banished to that place, but she's married to a bit of a tyrant who rules the roost, and what he says, goes!'

'Well, if you could write down Daniel Murphy's address, I could maybe talk to him.'

'I'll do that straight away.' She rose and opened a drawer in the dresser, took out a notepad and pen and wrote down the address. 'It's easy to find. Daniel's father runs a joinery business and timber yard with his sons, and they work together.'

I took the note, read it and shoved it in my pocket. 'Thank you, Mrs. Dunn. I'll see what I can do.'

'Bye, Robbie. You're a good lad. See you next time.' She handed over the bag of washing, waved goodbye and went inside as I left.

The brown paper parcel sat on the kitchen table. Mrs. Dunn sighed, untied the string, opened up the paper and took out the linen. Through tear-filled eyes, she crushed up and binned the brown paper, wound up the string and popped it into the dresser drawer.

Next morning, when I pulled up at the side door in the van, Agatha was in the process of stacking parcels on the step for me.

'Morning, Agatha,' I whispered as I lifted the packages.

'Morning,' she whispered back. 'I don't know your name.'

'Robbie.'

We carried a large basket filled with starched sheets for the hospital, to the van, and as we heaved it in, I mentioned, 'Amy has red hair and is pregnant, if that's any help.'

A nun appeared at the door and hovered, watching us.

Agatha mouthed, ok, then turned and hurried indoors.

I'd wondered if I should tell Ma and Da about Daniel, but decided to keep that to myself meantime. I had a plan.

On Sunday afternoon, I walked through town to the Murphy's address. The yard had always been there in my lifetime, but not needing to buy wood at my age, I hadn't been inside before.

J. Murphy & Sons Joiners and Timber Merchants was emblazoned on a sign above the shop, which was closed, like all the others in town, for the Sabbath. I had a wander around the outside into the timber yard. The sound of sawing could be heard and the fresh smell of resin and newly hewn wood filled my nostrils. I followed the sound past stacks of logs, planks of various sizes, bird tables and garden furniture for sale, until I came to a large shed with a man working just inside the open door. He had stopped sawing, so I stepped forward and tapping on the door, called out, 'Hello,' in greeting.

A tall guy with a firm, muscular body, dark curly hair and skin that looks tanned with rosy cheeks from working outside, turned towards me with a smile.

'Hi there. Can I help you?'

He looked a little older than me, so I guessed it could be Daniel.

'Er ... Are you Daniel?'

'Aye, that's me.' He laid down his saw. 'We're not meant to be open today.'

'My name is Robbie O'Sullivan. I drive a van for the Magdalene Laundry and I wanted to talk to you, er ... about ... er ... Amy.' I could feel my face going red.

'Amy? What do you know about Amy?' His face clouded. 'Tell me!'

I told him all that had happened – all that I knew, and waited for his response.

Daniel rubbed a hand through his hair. 'This is weird. Thank you for telling me this.

I'm horrified to think that Amy may be ill-treated – by nuns, of all people! He paced back and forth digesting the information. 'Are you able to go inside the laundry?'

'No, I just deliver and collect at a side door. Sometimes I need to go into the packaging room. I've seen through to the ironing place they have. Lots of girls are pounding away in clouds of steam. I told you about Agatha, so I'm hoping she's on duty tomorrow. She may have some news of Amy or whatever her name is now.'

'You might see her tomorrow?'

'Yes, unless they've put someone else on dispatch. Do you think we might be able to come up with some plan to get Amy out of the building?'

'To be sure, we can try.' Daniel went quiet for a moment. I've written to Amy every single week but I've never had any reply. I was thinking that she didn't want anything to do with me anymore.'

'Perhaps the nuns didn't give her your letters?'

'I'm beginning to wonder that myself. I'm so glad Mrs. Dunn gave you my address. She's a lovely, warm person. Mrs. O'Neill is a nice lady too. She never made me feel out of place in that big house.' He started pacing again. 'But Amy's father … he's just a pompous bully! Me and Amy wanted to marry. I could have supported her and our child, but Oh! No! He wasn't going to have his daughter marrying a tradesman! Amy's seventeen, for goodness' sake, but he treats her like a child.'

'Strange that he'd rather lose her altogether,' I muttered. 'Does your family know about Amy and er … the baby?'

'Yes, they do. My folks are very fond of her and were horrified when I told them what her father had done. They were in favour of us marrying. We're not a religious family, so it doesn't matter to them if we can't be married in a church.'

'When is the baby due?' I ventured.

'Any time now, I reckon. I've been worried sick wondering how she's going to cope as it doesn't look like her parents are going to take her home. Have you seen any children at this convent laundry?'

I shook my head and thought it best not to mention that I'd heard screams.' I could come back tomorrow night to let you know if the girl, Agatha, has any word of Amy?'

'That'd be good. Come about 7o'clock and I'll be in here.'

He shook my hand. 'Thanks, Robbie for all that you're doing. Call me Danny.'

'I'm concerned about Amy and I don't even know her, Danny. I have sisters I care about and can only imagine what you're going through. I'll see you tomorrow night then'.

Danny nodded and I set off for home.

Ruth

I've been kept on ironing duties for over a week and I prefer it to standing at the wash tubs with the big paddle. My legs and back ache but that is becoming normal. There is no set rota as the nuns liked to shift us around, from job to job, sometimes weeks on one chore, other times only a day, to keep us unsettled.

Agatha has been kept on in the dispatch bay but I miss her presence Although we hardly communicate, Agatha is always kind and gives me a wink or encouraging smile when she can.

When I'd ironed three batches of laundry for customers, I carried the bundles through to be packaged, as was the rule. Agatha was on duty and while handing over the fresh laundry, I felt that she was staring at my hair.

'What is it?' I mouthed.

Checking that no nuns were nearby, Agatha whispered, 'Are you Amy?'

Startled, I nodded. 'How do you know?'

'Someone was asking about you?'

'Was it Danny?'

'No, the van driver, Robbie.'

'I don't know a Robbie. Oh, maybe Mrs. Dunn got my note.'

A loud voice rang out, 'Here is someone to show you what happens when you disrespect the Sisters of Mercy.'

I jumped and turned to see the girl who had attacked the nun with the stool, limp into the room preceded by a gloating nun. The girl's head had been shaved. She looked ashen-faced and although wearing a loose shift, no longer looked pregnant. She had a plaster on her left arm and her legs were both bandaged.

'God in Heaven!' Agatha uttered under her breath.

The nun gave the girl a shove. 'Get moving, girl. You can work at a wash tub. You still have one good arm.'

Although she was being humiliated, the injured girl held her head up and stuck out her chin as she was marched away to be shown off to the other workers.

I hurried back to my ironing board and picked up the next piece of clothing and started pressing. Though horrified by what I'd just witnessed, my mind was assimilating the fact that someone was asking about me! I felt a little burst of joy and allowed a smile to linger on my lips.

Robbie

I decided that the next time I went to the O'Neill's residence, I would ask to speak with Mrs. O'Neill. I had a feeling that she would welcome her daughter home.

Meanwhile, I was delighted to see Agatha waiting at the door with the laundry packages for me. She smiled and walked over to the van as I opened the back doors., 'Good morning, Robbie. I've spoken with the girl you're looking for,' she said in hushed tones. 'She's called Ruth now.'

We lifted in the baskets, bags and parcels as usual while whispering without looking at each other.

'That's great. Tell her I've met Danny and we're hoping to get her out.'

'Oh, I wish I could get out of here too.' She sighed.

'Maybe you could both escape,' I suggested. 'Where would you go?'

'I don't know anyone. I was sent here because I was orphaned at thirteen.'

'No family at all?'

'None.'

'How old are you now?'

'Eighteen.'

My heart went out to this lovely girl. I stared at her sideways as I closed the van doors. She was very thin and her blonde hair was short and ragged. Her shift looked too big for her and she had bare feet in wooden clogs.

'Agatha! You're needed in packaging,' a nun called from the doorway.

'What's your real name?' I asked as I walked past her to the driver's door.

'Daisy,' came the reply as she hurried back to her duties.

'Daisy, Daisy,' I said to myself over and over as I drove around throughout the day. Daisy suits her so well. She is as pretty as the flower she's named after. I found myself singing, *'Daisy, Daisy give me your answer do, I'm half-crazy all for the love of you.'* I had a big grin on my face and customers commented on my cheerfulness.

When I returned to the laundry in the afternoon to drop off and collect more bags, Daisy was again the one to bring out the packages. My heart thumped noticeably in my chest when I saw her. *Good grief! I must be falling for her,* I thought.

She gave me a big smile. 'I've told Ruth ... Amy, about you seeing Danny. She's thrilled. Desperate to get out.'

'I'm meeting him tonight.'

We conducted the hand-over with no further chat as we knew we were being watched.

Before returning the van at the end of the day, I drove up to the big houses and pulled in at the O'Neill residence. The car wasn't there, so I hoped that Mr. O'Neill was still abroad. Mrs. Dunn was opening the side door as I walked towards it.

'I heard the van on the gravel. Is something wrong?'

'No, quite the opposite, I would say. May I come in?'

Mrs. Dunn stepped back and gestured for me to enter.

'I've spoken with Danny and I'm going to meet him again tonight. A girl who does the packaging at the moment, knows Amy.'

The housekeeper gasped. 'Oh, that's marvellous. Sit down, sit down. How is she?'

I only know that she's been renamed Ruth. Danny and I are hopefully going to help her, and possibly another girl, to escape.'

'Oh, by the way, have a look at this, Robbie. It came today.' Mrs. Dunn handed me a page from the weekly newspaper. 'I'm pretty sure that girl is Amy,' she said, pointing to a girl in a photograph of launderesses in the Magdalene Laundry. It's blurred of course but I'm sure it's her.'

'I'm not sure at all. I haven't seen anyone wearing a white cap and apron. That could be Agatha who I've told you about, standing next to the one you think is Amy, or Ruth as she's called."

'Ruth,' Mrs. Dunn tried out the name. 'But how will you manage to get them away?' she asked, returning to our earlier conversation.

'That's what we're going to plan tonight. I'm meeting Danny at seven. I wanted to speak to Mrs. O'Neill to see if we could bring Amy home. Is she in the house now?'

'I'll get her right away.' Mrs. Dunn replied and hurried from the kitchen.

She returned moments later with Amy's mother.

I stood up as they entered. 'Mrs. O'Neill, I hope you don't mind me dropping in like this, but I thought you should know that er, Danny and I are hoping to get your daughter away from the Magdalene Laundry as soon as we can.'

The woman was visibly trembling and near to tears.

'What we need to know is, will it be alright to bring Amy here?'

Mrs. O'Neill shook her head. 'My husband will forbid it. He won't have Amy in the house ever again.' She broke down and Mrs. Dunn helped her to a chair and gave her a handkerchief.

Mrs. O'Neill continued, 'I'll never understand him. He's become quite brutal and is only interested in status and money. I'm missing my daughter so much. I'm so worried about her … and the baby.' She held the handkerchief to her eyes and sobbed.

'I need to get the van back now, but rest assured that we'll do all we can to get Amy out of that place. I have an idea of where she could stay. Do you think you could quickly pack a bag for her with some things to wear as she just has a grey uniform shift?'

Amy's mother rose straight away. 'Yes, I'll be right back,' and she ran up the stairs.

She returned in a few minutes with a small suitcase. 'I've put in some underwear and a nightie, a pinafore and blouses that I hope won't be too tight. Toiletries and her hairbrush and sandals,' she added. 'I hope that will tide her over until we can buy her some new things.'

'I'm sure they will be just fine, thank you.'

Mrs. O'Neill grabbed my arm. 'M. My husband is returning tomorrow. Please don't let him find out about this.'

'It's ok, I'll just pass any message through Mrs. Dunn if that is alright with her?'

'Oh, of course, Robbie. You'd best go now and get the van back. You don't want the nuns to have any reason to be checking up on you,' replied the housekeeper.

Ruth

I'm lying on my mattress on the floor in the dormitory tonight, unable to sleep with excitement at the prospect of being free from this prison. Thoughts are going round and round in my head. *What is Danny planning? Where can I go? Does Mummy know about me? What about Daddy? Does he still hate me? What about the baby inside me? Will I be able to go to a hospital to have it?*

I want to speak with Agatha, but she is further up the room and I don't dare go to her as it would be the very time that a nun would come in to check up on us.

At breakfast, I manoeuvred beside her in the queue. 'Will you hear from Robbie today?'

She just shrugged and signalled with her eyes to move along.

After the usual bread and dripping breakfast and toilet break, a nun was waiting to give us our duties for the day.

'Ruth, you are taking in the bags of washing today and Agatha will show you how to separate the items and put the name tags on, then take them to the appropriate tub.

What luck! I will be near the door. Perhaps I'll even see this Robbie.

'The van won't be delivering the dirty linen for another hour or so yet, so you can get on with hanging out these sheets here,' she pointed to a loaded basket. 'There's a good wind today.' She turned away to the next girl.

My heart sank at the sight of the huge washing basket filled with wet linen.

As I stepped forward to attempt to lift the basket, Agatha moved beside me and we took a handle each and heaved the load out of the back door, before the nun noticed.

'Thanks Agatha. I don't think I could have lifted that on my own.'

'Your too far gone to be lifting anything. You could miscarry. Be very careful. Come on, I'll help you. That nun didn't say what I was to do until the dirty stuff was delivered, so I might as well help you.'

Between us, we lifted the basket over to the drying green and pegged out the sheets and pillow cases then shoved a clothes prop in the middle of the sagging clothes line.

'There's something very satisfying about seeing a line of washing blowing in the wind,' Agatha commented.

I nodded. *I hope I'll soon be seeing a row of white nappies on a line.*

'We could just walk out of the gate, couldn't we? No-one is out here,' I said looking around.

'That doesn't work. It's been tried many times before. The police just bring you back. I know, I've walked out myself in the past.'

'You have? What happened?'

'Well, I don't know my way around for a start, as I don't belong to this town. Then there's the dead give-away of the stylish, grey dress,' Agatha posed like a model. 'Then there's the fact that we are considered the lowest of the low, so I was just brought back and put in the cell. It's not worth it.'

I thought for a moment. 'What we need are proper clothes. Not these awful grey dresses. We could steal some of the laundry things we get in from the big houses,' I was getting excited. 'I know my way around. I'm sure Danny would help us both.'

'Forget it Ruth. You can't risk anything that might harm your baby. We better get inside before we are missed.'

Robbie

I walked briskly to Danny's yard, and sure enough, he was waiting.

'Hi Robbie. Let's have a talk in here.' He led me through a woodshed to the back wall where there was a table and chairs, phone and ledgers. 'Have a seat. This is where Da does his paperwork, but he's at the bowls tonight.'

'Do you have a plan then?' I asked.

'Well, I wondered if Amy could just walk out the door and get into your van?' he replied.

'Hmm, that's too risky. There could be a nun watching who'd prevent that. Besides, perhaps Amy would find it hard to climb up into the seat in the van.'

'Good point. Do you have any ideas?'

'I was wondering if she could somehow get into either a hospital basket, or one of the large cotton bags. It would be ideal if Agatha was on duty too and she could help lift her into the van. Oh, and by the way, her mother told me Amy could not go home. Her father won't allow it.' I paused. 'Would it be possible to take Amy to your house? What do you think your parents would say to that?'

'I think that's a great idea. I'm sure Ma would be delighted to have a girl to fuss over. Why don't we go and see her right now?'

I pursed my lips. 'Er … there's something else. Agatha, actually Daisy is her name, is also desperate to leave the Magdalene. Could we possibly take her as well? She could either climb into the back of the van, or sit up front with me. What do you think?'

'Well, it's a lot to ask of my Ma, but we'll see what she says Let's go!'

We marched off to the house, in anticipation.

Mrs. Murphy listened to our request, asked questions and I told her the little I knew of Daisy.

'Those poor girls. It's unimaginable in this day and age in the 1950s, that they are being so ill-used! Of course, they can both come here. I have that spare room up the stairs that has twin beds, as it happens. It used to be for the two boys when they were young, but Daniel has his own room now and of course, Ryan is married and has his own house round the corner. I'll get it all freshened up tomorrow.'

'Thanks so much, Ma,' said Danny giving her a squeeze. 'You're the best!'

'I know,' she laughed. 'Actually, it will be lovely to have two young ladies here instead of men.'

Danny and I made some further plans with the intention of freeing the girls in four days' time.

When I drew up at the door this morning, a nun came out with a different girl. She looked pregnant.

'Ruth, grab one of these bags of washing and take it inside. Agatha will show you what to do.

Ruth? This must be Amy!

I hurried forward to help the girl carry the heavy bag to the door. The nun put out an arm before I could help her take it over the step. 'Leave her to do it herself, young man. You can get on with bringing in the rest.' She didn't move.

'I can't let a lady in her condition lift such a weight,' I said, and heaved the bag onto the step. Amy gave me a grateful look.

The nun was taken aback and just stood aside and let me past.

'Thanks,' I said. 'I'll just bring in the other bags,' and flashed her a big smile.

I carried the washing in and dumped the bags in a pile. 'Would you like me to do anything else to help?

The nun looked flustered. 'No thank you, young man. That's quite enough.'

'I'll be on my way then,' I replied, giving her a grin. 'Bye for now, Sister.'

'Good bye,' she replied coyly.

I hope I've charmed her enough to prevent her giving Amy and Daisy a hard time.

I called at the O'Neill's home on the morning of the planned escape.I noticed that all the blinds were down, which was unusual.

'Mrs. Dunn opened the door to me. 'Oh, Robbie. Something terrible has happened. Mr. O'Neill has died!'

'What?'

'Yes. A heart attack. We heard two days ago.'

I was just standing there with my mouth open.

'Poor Mrs. O'Neill. She's in shock. I know they weren't all that happy latterly,' she rushed on,' but they *have* been married for twenty years.'

'Oh, how awful,' I said lamely. 'When is the funeral?'

'That has still to be arranged. His body hasn't been brought home yet. It's expected tomorrow.

Poor Mrs. O'Neill and poor wee Amy.' She dabbed her eyes.

'Well, we have arranged to take Amy to the Murphy's home, you'll be pleased to hear. Mrs. Murphy is happy about it and it looks like Amy will be able to return here soon after all.'

'When are you hoping to get her away/'

'This morning,' I replied. 'And, I'm hoping we can rescue one other girl as well. Mrs. Murphy is happy to take her in too. Her name is Daisy and she's an orphan.'

'This morning! Oh, my goodness! I must tell the mistress."

'Yes, I'd better get on my way and hope that Amy is ready. I told our plans to Daisy, the girl who's leaving with her. I'll be in touch. Pass on my condolences to Mrs. O'Neill.'

Ruth

I can hardly wait for the van man to come this morning. Agatha is still in the packing bay and I'm still at the steam pressing, so we should be able to stick to the plan. I have only a few more pieces to do for the boarding houses, so I'll soon be able to take them through next door.

I carried my linen to the packing room where Agatha was wrapping clothes in brown paper. She nodded down at my clogs, indicating that I remove them so I slipped them off and shoved them with a foot, away under the packing table. She then signalled to me to go over near the door where there was a large calico bag lying open. I placed all the bedlinen and tablecloths inside it as normal, then looking around, saw that Agatha was occupying a nun with something. I jumped inside the bag and pulled the flap over me.

Moments later, Agatha walked over and tied the tapes closed above me. 'All good,' she whispered.

It was only a few minutes before the laundry van drew up outside. I heard the nun open the door and order Agatha to take the parcels out to the step. 'Young man, will you carry these bags for the boarding houses to your van and pick up these parcels too. Agatha will help you.'

I listened to the footsteps go back and forth, then felt myself being lifted up in the laundry bag and carried outside. I thudded down on the floor of the van, quite comfortably and next thing I knew, the doors were slammed and the engine started.

To my surprise, the tapes above me were loosened and Agatha's face appeared as the bag was opened. She helped me to sit up.

'Gosh, you managed it,' I exclaimed.

'Yes, I can hardly believe it. The nun went indoors and I just jumped in the back of the van!' We had to stifle our glee.

'We'd only travelled a short distance when the van stopped and Robbie came around and opened one of the doors slightly. 'Everyone ok?'

'Yes,' we whispered in unison.

'I'm meeting Danny here where it's quiet. He's bringing the works van to pick you both up and take you to his folks' home.'

Just at that, Danny pulled up in his joiner's van. 'Sorry I'm a bit late, but I had something to do first,' he explained. 'Where's Amy?'

He caught sight of me inside the back of the van and ran over to give me a hug.

'My darling girl, whatever have they done to you?' He stroked my face. 'Your beautiful hair! How's the baby?' I saw him looking at my clothes, my red, rough hands with broken nails and my bare feet.

The baby's fine as far as I know. I'm just so glad to be out of that place. By the way, this is Agatha, no, I mean, Daisy. Oh, Danny, thank you, thank you,' and I burst into tears.

'Let's just get you home,' he said, lifting me carefully into the long front passenger seat of his van. 'Now you, Daisy,' and he lifted her too. 'There's room for you both in the front.'

Robbie handed him the suitcase for Amy, then drove off to do his deliveries.

The Murphys

'Oh, goodness me, let's get you both inside. Daniel, carry Amy, she has no shoes.'

Mrs. Murphy fussed around the girls and got them both seated in the comfy armchairs in the living room. Danny sat on the chair arm and cradled Amy.

'This is my husband, John,' she explained to Daisy, as the man came into the room carrying two blankets. He handed them to his wife who tucked them around the girls.

'I'm shocked to see you is such a state, Amy,' he said, shaking his head. 'Your beautiful hair! And you're so thin! What of the baby, is that alright, lass?'

'I hope so. The nuns cut off everyone's hair. I suppose it's to make us feel humiliated, and it certainly does! But that's not the half of it. We were starved and beaten and put in a room like a cell, as well as being worked like slaves in the laundry!'

'Hush now, what would you like first? A hot bath or something to eat?' Mrs. Murphy intervened.

'Something to eat please,' both girls chorused.

'How does ham and eggs with some toast and marmalade sound?'

'Heavenly,' sighed Amy.

'With a huge pot of tea,' added Daisy.

Later, once the girls had been thoroughly spoiled and could not eat another morsel, Mrs. Murphy said, 'I'm off to run a bath. You can have one first, Amy, then I'll run one for you, Daisy.' She left the room to go upstairs to the bathroom.

Amy smiled over to Danny. 'Could I have my case over please? I'll see what Mummy put in for me.'

Danny lifted the case on to the floor at her feet and opened the lid.

'How lovely to have my own clothes again. I think the blouses will still fit me as I'm so skinny, apart from my baby bump,' she laughed. 'That pinafore dress looks big enough. Oh, good, there's underwear and two nighties. I can give one to you, Daisy.'

Mrs. Murphy returned. 'Right lass. Let's get you upstairs and into the bath.'

Once Amy was luxuriating in the hot water and scented bubbles, Mrs. Murphy came back down to the living room.

The men were looking serious while chatting with Daisy.

'It's appalling what those lassies have had to put up with,' growled John Murphy.

'I know, but let's not discuss it any more now. I'm sure Daisy just wants to be free from it all' Turning to the young girl, she said,' I think a good long sleep after your baths is in order for you both.'

Daisy nodded in agreement. 'I feel so cosy and comfortable and, and … safe,' she struggled to explain. A tear trickled down her cheek. 'Thank you so, so much for your kindness.' Her words and look encompassed them all.

'Now, what are we going to do about clothes for you, Daisy,' Mrs. Murphy briskly got back to the business in hand.

'Amy said I could wear one of her nighties,' Daisy answered.

Danny shoved the case towards his mother.

'That's sorted for now then,' she said closing the suitcase and carrying it upstairs.

Robbie

When I went back to the laundry later in the morning to drop off more soiled linen and collect the latest deliveries, I felt my stomach turning over with nerves. What if someone had seen what happened?

The same nun who'd been there previously was placing packages on the step for me as I got out of the van. I smiled to her. 'Hello, Sister. I'll just bring in the bags,' and I started to unload the laundry.

'Did you see Agatha this morning?' she snapped.

'Yes. Why, is something wrong? She helped me with the bags as usual.'

'Well, she's gone. Seems that Ruth has gone with her. They must have run out of the gate. Stupid girls. They won't get far. Especially Ruth in her big clogs,' she added with a laugh. 'The garda will catch them.'

'Oh, not so good. Would you like me to keep a look out for them?'

'Well, if you see them boy, bring them back here.' she turned and swept indoors, leaving me to carry on with my work.

'I will certainly *not* be doing that,' I murmured.

'You did *what?*' my Da said, eyes wide. 'You're telling me that you and Danny Murphy kidnapped these girls and took them away from their home and work!' He started pacing the kitchen floor. 'And they're staying at the Murphy's?'

'We didn't exactly kidnap them Da. They were desperate to escape from a terrible life at the laundry. You wait 'til you see the state of them. The nuns shaved off their hair and practically starved them.'

'You could end up in court over all of this, me boy, and what of your degree course then?'

'I don't think the university will be interested.'

'Oh, no? They'll need to know if you're in prison,' he shouted.

'Who's going to prison?' Ma asked. 'I could hear your raised voices from the yard.'

'It might be me'laddo here,' he declared, pointing at me. 'Wait till you hear what he's been and done now!'

Amy

'I don't remember ever having such a good sleep,' said Daisy, stretching and smiling to me on Monday morning. 'A proper bed, sheets, blankets *and* an eiderdown. Luxury!' she declared. 'After five years in that workhouse, I'd forgotten what a bedroom was like!'

'Yes, it's wonderful to be in a proper bed again instead of a thin mattress on the floor,' I agreed. 'However, I haven't forgotten my lovely bedroom at home'. *Though will I ever be allowed back there again!* 'I can smell bacon! I can't believe the amount of food we ate at tea last night.' I threw back the bedclothes and sat up.

'Are you awake, girls? Mrs. Murphy was outside the door. 'Can I come in?

'Of course,' we chorused.

'Here are a couple of dressing gowns for you just now, until I can get new. One is mine,' and she handed it to Daisy, 'and the other is an old one of John's, but it's clean,' she added as she laid it on my bed. Come down for some breakfast and we'll have a chat about what we're going to do. John is already away to work, but Daniel has stayed back meantime.'

We were downstairs within five minutes.

The breakfast dishes had just been cleared away, when we heard a knock at the door.

'Mm, I wonder who this is?' Mrs. Murphy walked across the room. 'Oh, it's you, Robbie, come away in. The girls have just had breakfast. Would you like some tea?'

'I'd love some, thanks. Hi Danny, morning ladies.'

'What brings you here this morning?'

'Well, I'm afraid that I bring some sad news, er … for Amy.'

I straightened up, 'What is it Robbie? Have I to go back to the Magdalene?'

'No, No, nothing like that. But bad news. I'm sorry to have to tell you that your father has died.'

I don't know what I felt at that moment. Shock? Yes. Grief? No. Numbness? Yes.

Mrs. Murphy and Daisy both rushed over to put their arms around me. Danny rose and stood behind me with his hands on my shoulders.

'Oh, you poor lamb, as if you haven't been through enough,' Mrs. Murphy said.

'My dear friend, I know what it's like to lose a father too. Don't worry, we'll look after you,' said Daisy, giving my hand a squeeze. Danny was silent.

'What happened, Robbie?' I asked.

'As far as I know, he had a heart attack and died on Thursday. He's being brought home this week. Your mother doesn't know when the funeral will be yet.'

'That awful man who put me in that hellish place is really dead?' I asked. They were all taken aback by my reaction. 'Well, there *is* justice after all.'

Mrs. Murphy tried to comfort me. 'You're just in shock dear. Don't speak like that of your father.'

I ignored her and sat in silence with my thoughts. *I will be able to go home now surely? I suppose Mummy will miss him, but he broke my heart when he threw me out. He disowned me. I will not go to the funeral.*

I became aware of the others speaking but I didn't hear them.

'Robbie, would you take a message to my mother please?

'Of course.'

'Tell her that I am sorry for her loss. Tell her that I know he was my father, but I am not going to the funeral. Besides, it would be awkward for her if people were to see me in my condition. Ask her if she would make an arrangement to visit me here?'' I looked at Mrs. Murphy for approval and she nodded with a small smile. 'Tell her that I'd like to come home and that I love her and miss her.'

Robbie nodded, 'I will have a delivery for her this afternoon, so I'll certainly pass on your message. I'll let you know what she says as soon as I can.'

Danny led me over to the settee. 'Sit down and just let the news sink in. This must be an awful shock.' He sat beside me and stroked my hands.

'I can feel our baby kicking,' he smiled, gently touching my tummy.'

Mrs. Murphy appeared shrugging into her coat. 'I'm just going to nip around to the surgery to see if Dr Moore will call in to see you.' She pulled her hat firmly onto her head, slipped her hands into gloves and turning to me said, 'He won't say anything, don't worry. I'll be back soon.' She gave Danny a knowing look and left.

'Oh, Danny, what if he makes me go back to that place,' I burst out.

'Sh, my love. It'll be alright. There's something I have for you.' He felt in his pocket and brought out a velvet ring box which he opened. 'Here, put this on,' he whispered with a smile.

I stared in amazement at a beautiful gold wedding ring. 'But, but …'

'It's alright. A bit back-to-front I admit, but as far as anyone outside of the family is concerned, we are married. We'll do it properly as soon as possible; that's if you'll have me?' he added.

'Yes, yes,' I gasped as he slipped the gold band on my finger.

'It is just a little bit big, but I don't think it will slip off,' I said.

Daisy rushed to kiss me. 'Oh, how wonderful. You mustn't feel ashamed anymore.'

'Ma, Da and I discussed it, and as far as the doctor is concerned, you are Mrs. Murphy. I bought the ring before I met you yesterday. That's why I was a bit late in arriving,' Danny explained.

Robbie

Nothing untoward happened when I did my usual shifts at the laundry and I felt happy to be able to pass on the message to Mrs. O'Neill from Amy.

'How is she, lad?' asked Mrs. Dunn as she let me in through the side door. 'What a time we are having, to be sure.'

'Amy is being well cared for, Mrs. Dunn and I have a message for her mother, if I could see her please?'

'I'll just get her. Have a seat.' She disappeared through the hallway but returned straight away with Mrs. O'Neill.

'You have word from Amy for me?' her hand clutched to her chest.

I told her what Amy had asked me to relay to her and tears came into her eyes. 'Of course, she can come back here whenever she likes.' She wiped her eyes with a lacy handkerchief. 'I understand if she doesn't want to come to the funeral.' She thought for a moment. 'I would love to visit her at Mr. and Mrs. Murphy's home. Do you think it would be alright for me to see her this afternoon?'

'I'm sure that'll be fine, but I'll call in and let Danny's mother know to expect you. If I don't come back within an hour, you'll know that it will be okay.'

Amy

Mummy arrived promptly at 2o'clock. Oh, it was so lovely to see her and to have a big hug. Mrs.

Murphy passed on her sincere condolences. She had the best china out and a fruit cake sliced and ready to be served.

'I'm so shocked at the state of you,' said Mummy, fingering my scrappy hair and stroking my hands. 'Your poor little hands. They are so red and dry. Oh! she gasped when she saw the ring.'

'It's okay Mummy. Danny has given me this ring so that people will think we are married. Mrs. Murphy called a doctor in to see me this morning. It all worked out so well, as it wasn't even the usual one.

Mummy looked towards Mrs. Murphy, who explained, 'Dr Moore's on holiday for a month to visit his sister in Canada, so it was a locum who came out. He took it for granted that Amy was married and has booked her into the maternity hospital'.

'He gave me a row for not having been to him earlier but he seemed nice. He said I was a bit underweight but presumed that I'd probably had a lot of morning sickness. I didn't contradict him. I've to eat lots of good food and he thinks I'll have the baby within two weeks.'

'That's wonderful. I take it that you and Danny plan to marry?' Mummy asked.

'Oh yes, just as soon as possible. He went to work and thought it was best if I saw you on my own just now, but he wants me to assure you that he'll be there for me and the baby.'

Mummy turned as Daniel's mother handed her a cup and saucer and linen napkin.

'Thank you, and thank you so very much for your kindness in taking Amy in. She'll be able to come home soon though.' And she looked to me expectantly.

'Amy is welcome here as long as she likes, but I know she'll be wanting home to her own bed,' Mrs. Murphy said.

'I'll come home as soon as the funeral is over and done with,' I told Mummy.

'I've brought you some more clothes and things,' she indicated a bag at her feet 'and I'll give Mrs. Murphy some money for your keep.'

'There's no need for that,' Mrs. Murphy replied, handing Mummy and me some fruit cake.

'We'll come to some arrangement,' said Mummy, taking a bite of cake. 'Mm, this is delicious.'

Just at that, there was a tap on the living room door, which opened and Daisy came in. She was still wearing the dressing gown.

'Come away in, dear,' said Mrs. Murphy, pouring out another cup.

'Mummy, this is Daisy. Robbie and Danny helped her to escape along with me.'

Daisy and Mummy smiled to each other.

'It's good to meet you Daisy. I believe you have been a very good friend to my daughter.'

Daisy gave me a grin. 'We've been friends to each other, haven't we?' she answered. 'I thought I'd give you some peace to talk, but I heard the tea cups clinking and hope it's alright to come in.'

'I'm going to take the bus into Bray tomorrow morning to buy clothes for Daisy and I'll be delighted to buy anything that Amy needs too,'

Mrs. Murphy declared as she handed Daisy her tea and cake.

'Oh, that is so good of you,' Daisy mumbled between mouthfuls. 'We can have a measuring session later.'

'I'll buy you a couple of nice maternity dresses,' Mummy said to me. 'I think I'll just go into town when I leave here and see what there is. Is it okay if I come back in the morning, Mrs. Murphy?'

'Of course. Come around any time, and please call me Bernie, short for Bernadette,' she added.

'Thank you, Bernie. I'm Concepta. I've enjoyed the tea and cake, but I'm eager to go and buy some clothes for Amy, and perhaps some baby things, so I'll get off now and see you all again in the morning. Take care, darling.' Mummy gave me a big hug and kiss and left soon after.

'I'm so pleased for you that your mother is happy to see you again and she seems excited about the baby,' Mrs. Murphy said.

Mummy arrived again next morning, loaded with packages. Daisy and I were alone in the house as the men were at work and Mrs. Murphy was in Bray.

'Here are two dresses for you to try,' she said, handing me a large carrier bag. 'And there are some maternity undies in this bag too,' she whispered. 'Now, I've ordered a cot and high pram to be delivered to the house at the end of this week, along with a baby bath, cot covers and just wait 'til you see these,' she beamed as she produced a pile of beautiful white nappies and baby garments which we all oohed and aahed over.

'Oh, Mummy, you've gone mad! Thank you so much for all of this. And you've ordered a pram and cot?' I marvelled at the gifts.

'I'm just sorry that you haven't been able to choose them yourself, but you and Daniel will be able to buy all the other things that your baby needs. I still have your crib with its white broderie anglaise frills, in the attic, along with the high chair you used as a little one. You can have those if you like. There are probably some toys as well. Mrs. Dunn and I will have a search.'

'It's all so exciting!' exclaimed Daisy.

I had to agree, but I was becoming quite nervous about the birth.

Daniel

This has been a really weird time. I'm so glad that Amy is safe and away from the Magdalene Laundry. My folks have been great and Ma came back from Bray today with a wardrobe of clothes for Daisy as well as some baby clothes.

I'm going to go to the Registry Office to enquire about the procedure for getting wed.

Robbie is keen to make an official complaint to the Council about the treatment in the laundry, but I'm not happy to do that just yet. Not until Amy and I are married.

I've been thinking about perhaps moving away after that. I could start up a business on my own. I'll have a talk with Dad and Amy tonight.

Robbie

'Ma, I have had no repercussions at the laundry. No-one suspects that I had anything to do with the girls' disappearance. I just wish I could do more to stop all this terrible ill-treatment of the workers. I want to make a formal complaint about the nuns, but Danny asked me to wait a while until he and Amy are married and settled. He seems to have his heart set on having his own joinery business somewhere else where no-one knows them.'

'To be sure, that would be a good idea. A fresh start for them,' Ma agreed. 'What about Daisy? What are her plans, do you know?

'I'm going out to meet Daisy soon so we can go for a walk and a chat. It'll be a bit more private. Besides, Danny wants to have a talk with his Da about getting married and the business, and moving away and all that.'

'They certainly have a lot on their plates,' said Ma. 'John and Bernie have been wonderful, taking the girls in and they'll be concerned for their son and Amy just now.'

'I'll get away now then. See you later on. Bye, Ma.'

'Bye son. Say hello to Daisy from me.'

I walked to the Murphy's house and Mrs. Murphy welcomed me in.

'Good to see you, Robbie. Daisy is so excited to be going out with you.'

Daisy came into the living room. I saw her cheeks turning pink with embarrassment.

'Mrs. Murphy! I'm not *excited*. I'm just pleased to be able to go out again.'

I felt slightly quashed.

'You are looking nice, Daisy,' I said, admiring her new dress.

'Thank you, kind sir,' she replied. 'I have new shoes and stockings and this lovely coat,' she posed to show me a smart blue coat and pointed a foot to show off black patent shoes. 'Mrs. Murphy has been amazing, buying lots of lovely things for me.'

Mrs. Murphy smiled. 'It was a great pleasure, my dear. I've never had a girl to buy pretty things for so I've enjoyed myself. I'm just so pleased that everything fits and you are happy.'

'Well, we'll be off then. I won't be late home,' said Daisy as we went to the door.

'Have a good time, dear. Bye, Robbie, Bye Daisy.

'Where would you like to go for a walk?' I asked.

'I've no idea, really. I don't know this area,' Daisy replied.

We wandered along the road in an awkward silence. There was no wind on this mild evening and the first leaves of autumn were drifting quietly down.

'We could have a stroll in the park or go window shopping or go down to the river and watch the boats,' I suggested.

'Mm, I'd like to go to a park. The trees are lovely just now. Is there a duck pond and swings? That's a memory I have from when I was little,' Daisy replied with shining eyes.

'Your wish is my command m'lady. To the swings and the duckpond we shall go.'

We made our way to the local park which was almost deserted apart from a few dog walkers. Daisy was thrilled to be out in the open and we spent some time watching a noisy squad of mallards being fed by an elderly gentleman.

'Next time, we must bring some bread for them,' decided Daisy.

'I agree. Feeding ducks is one of life's greatest pleasures.' I replied, feeling rather pleased that she felt there would be another time.

We wandered along paths around flower beds chatting amiably.

'What are your plans?' I asked. 'Have you thought about a job?'

'Yes, I have, as a matter of fact. I haven't mentioned it to anybody yet, but I'd like to train as a nurse. I know what it's like to be ill-treated, so I'd like to be able to help people feel safe and comforted, especially when they are ill or frightened.'

'I think that's a marvellous idea. Have you made any enquiries at a hospital yet?

'No, but I'll do that soon. I am going to have a chat about it with Mr. and Mrs. Murphy and hopefully, they'll let me stay with them, unless I need to go into a nurses' residence.'

'There are two hospitals quite nearby. I know, as I've been delivering the laundry obviously.'

Daisy nodded. 'What are *you* going to do? That is just a summer job, isn't it?'

'Yes. Next week, I'm going back to university for my final year.'

'Oh, that sounds very important. What are you hoping to do when you graduate?

'Well, I'm not completely sure yet, perhaps teaching, but I think I'd also like to get into journalism. Maybe writing a column in a newspaper? Could be part-time. I'd really like to be able to bring all the dreadful happenings in the Magdalene Laundry to the public's attention, for starters.'

'Wow, that would be so good. Oh, look. there are swings! Please can I have a shot on one?' Daisy's face lit up and we ran to the swings. We laughed and larked around like kids and thoroughly enjoyed ourselves.

It seemed perfectly natural to hold hands as we walked back to the Murphy's house.

Amy

Dear Mrs. Dunn,

I hope you are well.

I'm feeling very mixed up at the moment. Much as I love being at the Murphy's house, I so miss my mother (and you). It's the funeral today, so hopefully, I shall be able to go home soon. I feel guilty that I don't have any grief for my father. He disowned me when he could have helped me. Daniel has officially asked me to marry him and of course, I said I would. The banns have to be up for three weeks at the Registry Office so we should be able to wed soon. I'm feeling fat and uncomfortable and have been getting sharp pains now and again. Mrs. Murphy says that it's the baby practising. Maybe I'll have it before we can get married. I'm excited and worried at the same time!

I'm glad that Mummy has you to look after her. I hope to see you soon.

Love Amy x

Daniel

'Well, things are looking good. Dad has agreed to give me my share of the profits from the business and I've been to see an excellent property in Sanderton. It's only ten miles away so we'll be near to our friends and families. I thought we could both go and have a look around the place tomorrow. What do you say?'

'Oh, that sounds marvellous!' exclaimed Amy. 'Tell me all about it.'

'Well, there is a nice cottage, two bedrooms, living room, kitchen and bathroom. It has an enclosed garden, so that will be good for our baby.'

'Is it in the centre of the town?'

'Yes, it is, which will be good for business. The house is set back from the road though, so it will be quiet.'

'That sounds great,' said Amy, grinning. 'I can't wait to see it.'

'There is a shop which I thought we could develop as a hardware store, but I'll have to take someone on to work in that meanwhile. Then there is a large yard with two huge sheds.' Danny carried on breathlessly, his eyes shining. 'I can have a workshop and an office and the yard will be perfect for the timber.'

'Oh, Danny, it's all so exciting.' Then Amy had a thought. 'Will ours be the only timber and hardware business in the town?'

'Yes, I've already looked into that. Apart from Da's business, we will be the only other one in the county. It's perfect.'

Amy

'Are we nearly at the hospital?' I gasped. 'The pains are coming closer together.'

'I'm driving as fast as I can. It's only minutes away now. Hold on darling.' Daniel's knuckles were white as he gripped the steering wheel.

'I can see the hospital signs now, thank goodness. Oh, here's another pain starting.' The rest was all a bit of a blur. I can remember Danny pulling up at the main door, jumping out of the car and shouting for help. He ran beside the wheelchair as a nurse pushed me hurriedly along to a ward.

Through my haze of pain, I heard a voice direct Danny, 'Out of here, young sir. Go to the waiting area. This is no place for a man.'

'It's a boy,' was the next thing I remember. 'You've done really well. The birth was quick and straightforward. A 6lb baby. Shall I let your husband in?'

'Yes, please,' I smiled to the midwife. 'Thank you.'

'Hello, darling. How are you both?' Danny whispered as he gave me a kiss. 'You look exhausted.'

'We're fine, but both tired as you can see,' I said, indicating the sleeping child in the crib next to my bed.

'I can't wait to see him,' Danny said as he edged close to the new arrival. 'Oh, he's just perfect. May I hold him?'

'No, you may not, young man,' came the stern reprimand from a nurse who came bustling in through the door. 'I'm going to take baby away to the nursery now. He needs to sleep, and so does your wife. You can come back at visiting time tonight and you'll be able to have a cuddle with your son then.'

She pushed the cradle on wheels out of the room and Danny made a grimace and mouthed, 'Tyrant' to me. 'I better go, darling, but I'll be back in later. You get some sleep.' He added, 'Mum,' with a smile.

Daniel

'Amy's had a little boy. I'm a Dad!' I yelled and punched the air. 'I've been to tell my folks and they are so delighted.'

Robbie grinned and thumped me on the back. 'Congratulations, Daddy. How is Amy?'

'Tired, but seems to be fine. I wasn't allowed to stay with her but I'll see them both again tonight. I'll go up to Amy's mother's place now and let her have the good news.'

'Great. Give Amy my love and I'll pass on the news to my folks. Do you have a name yet?'

'Not finalised, but we'll be able to talk later. I must go now. See you soon.' I waved and drove off to my next important visit.

Amy

'How are you feeling tonight, darling?' asked Daniel as he slipped into the ward bearing flowers and gifts.

'Sore, tired but very happy,' I answered. 'Come and see your son. He's just been fed and is contented. He has a good pair of lungs. You should have heard him earlier when he was hungry!'

'Am I allowed to lift him?' Daniel asked.

'Yes, it's ok. I checked with the nurse before visiting.'

'I'll be very gentle,' murmured Daniel as he lifted the baby into his arms. 'He's beautiful, just like his mother. What are we going to call him? Do you have a preference?'

'Well, I would like to call him Robert after Robbie. If it hadn't been for him, I just can't imagine what it would have been like if I'd given birth in that awful place.'

'I completely agree,' answered Daniel. 'Robert it is then. Shall we call him Robbie, Rob, Bobby, Bert or Robert? he laughed.

'Let's make it, Robbie, and how about John for a middle name, after your father? Your parents have been so good to me, taking me into their home?'

Daniel nodded. 'Robert John Murphy. That sounds like a good strong name.'

'Did you tell Mummy?' I asked.

'Oh, yes. I almost forgot. She will come in soon. She wanted to give us some time on our own first. She was so thrilled and relieved that you were both ok. My mum and Daisy would like to visit tomorrow afternoon. They'll do the same. Just coming in for a short while after the first half hour.'

'That will be so good, oh, here's Mummy now,' I said, smiling as my mother appeared around the door, looking anxiously along the beds for me.

'Hello, dear,' she hurried over and gave me a kiss and stroked my arm.' Hello Daniel. 'Oh, look at this little cherub. He's gorgeous.'

'Would you like to hold your grandson, Robbie?' asked Daniel.

'Robbie?' she enquired, as she cradled him in her arms.

'Yes, Robert John, but we'll call him Robbie after our good friend.'

'That is a very good choice.'

Daniel

'Hello my two darlings,' I greeted Amy and Robbie next day. 'How are you both? Mum and Daisy are excitedly waiting to see you.'

'We are doing well, Danny. I was shown how to bath Robbie this morning and he is taking his feeds, so it's all good. It's hard trying to change his nappy and get him into clothes, but I'll be in here for ten days, so should be an expert by the time we come home.'

Just at that, a nurse came into the ward accompanied by a policeman.

'The Garda! Oh, no!' gasped Amy. 'They're coming over here.'

'Don't worry. Just keep calm,' I said, smiling and trying to sound confident.

'This officer would like a word, Mr. and Mrs. Murphy,' stated the nurse, drawing the curtain around the bed.

'I won't keep you long,' said the policeman. 'I am just following up some enquiries. I am looking out for an Amy O'Neill who escaped from the Magdalene Laundry convent some weeks ago, but I understand you are Amy Murphy, is this correct?' he asked, looking at Amy.

'Yes,' she answered smoothly. 'I am Amy Murphy.' She held out her left hand to show her wedding ring.

'Ah, well, I seem to have the wrong person.' He gave Amy a knowing look as he put away his notebook. 'The young lady in question was single. The nuns didn't have any information about her. She'll be miles away by now. I'll bid you goodbye and wish you and your husband and baby all the best.'

He gave me a wink and turned and left.

A nurse rustled in and pulled back the curtains. 'What did he want then?' she enquired.

'Oh, it was just a case of mistaken identity,' I answered and smiled as Ma and Daisy entered the room.

Danny and Amy were married soon after and lived at the O'Neill house while the premises in

Sanderton were being renovated. They have two children now and a thriving business.

Daisy married me after she completed her nursing training. We have two girls, Julie and Josie.

I am an English teacher at our local secondary school but have tirelessly campaigned for the closure of Magdalene Laundries throughout the country. I write part-time for our local paper, so that has been a good vehicle for the cause. Sadly, the Church and local government refuse to enter into any dialogue but I will continue to interview past workers and anyone who is willing to relate their stories.

Author's note
The Magdalene Laundry in Dublin was closed down in 1970. However, it was not until 1996 that the last laundry of that name was closed in England.

Café Dreams

The bus was pulling away from the bus stop as I hurried round the corner, head down against the driving rain. "Oh, no. Now I'll have half an hour to put off," I muttered, annoyed that I hadn't made sure of catching it. Looking around, I noticed a cafe across the road. *Haven't been in that one before. I might as well have a coffee and dry off a bit.*

I ran across the wet road, dodging cars and puddles and pushed open the door to the Café Dreams. It was bright, noisy and busy inside from what I could see through my steamed-up specs. I made my way over to the counter.

"Oh, hello, Jack. What a day! Your usual Americano and hot milk?" announced the cheerful proprietor.

"Er, thanks. Yes," I stammered, trying to peer over the top of my glasses. *How does he know me? I don't think I've seen him before.*

"I'm afraid your favourite table is taken by a young lady," the man continued, gesturing over to a corner, "but there is one seat left there beside her if you'd like it."

I nodded, paid, thanked him for the coffee and carried it towards the corner table. Edging past the other chairs trying not to bump into people, I was also manoeuvring a carrier bag containing a gift for my young nephew. *Am I imagining this or are people smiling to me?* I smiled back and arrived at the table occupied by a young woman.

The pretty brunette I could see as a blur smiled also and hurriedly lifted her coat and bag off a chair so I could sit down.

"Thank you," I acknowledged and laying down the tray, took off my wet coat. I hung this over the back of my chair and sat down, lifting my coffee cup and hot milk while the woman made room for my things. "Oh, I didn't get a spoon or serviette," I said looking around for somewhere to lay the tray.

'You can have this spoon. I didn't use it and I have a heap of paper napkins here. I always seem to need more than one, so you're welcome to these too," she smiled as she handed them over.

Shoving the tray down between my right calf and the table leg, I placed the carrier bag on the floor at my other side. "Thanks. That'll save me having to battle my way back to the counter again," I said, wishing my glasses would clear. I gave them a rub.

Turning my attention to the coffee, I took a few tentative sips of the hot liquid.

"You are Jack Cameron, aren't you?"

I jerked the cup and managed to spill coffee on the table.

"Oops, sorry," she said mopping up the splashes. "I've been reading your book and it's great," she chattered on. "I recognised you from your photograph on the back"'

Book! Photograph!

"My book?" I must have looked dumb.

"Yes, *Journey to the Dawn.* I've only just started it and I have it with me."

"You have it?"

She fumbled in her shopper and brought out a new paperback. "I'm sorry I couldn't come to your book signing on Saturday. I had to work, but I managed to buy the paperback version. You must be pleased," she beamed. "The man said the hardbacks were all sold out."

"Book signing?" I stumbled out. *What's going on here? I seemed unable to conduct a normal conversation.*

"You seem surprised," she carried on. "Here you are, looking serious and authorly on the back." She turned the paperback towards me.

Sure enough. The photograph on the back was definitely me. I just nodded and smiled. I became aware of the people at the next table nudging and whispering and looking in our direction. *That is the story I've written ... but I haven't had it accepted by a publisher yet. Have I stepped into some future version of me?* "Would you like me to sign it for you?" I asked with a sudden brainwave.

"Oh, that would be great," came the reply. "Just make it to Claire, thanks."

I opened up the front pages and quickly looked to see who the publisher was and mentally noted the name. *Yikes, it is next year's date! How weird is this!* Hurriedly turning to the blank front page, I wrote *Best wishes to Claire, Jack Cameron* and closed it over. I held the book for a moment and gazed at the cover. *The illustration is just as I imagined I'd like it. What is going on here?*

"Thank you so much ... Jack," Claire said with a shy smile. "I've never known a real live author before." She dropped the book back into her shopping bag. "Have you already started on another story or a sequel?"

"Em … not just yet. I'm having a rest." *If only!* "But I expect I'll be back to it soon," I replied and took a gulp of my coffee.

"Well, I must be going. It's been great to meet you and perhaps I'll see you in here again. I usually pop in on Fridays."

"Em … good to meet you too. Oh, and thanks for buying the book."

"No probs. I look forward to reading it." She stood to put on her coat, then squeezed past me. "I'll tell you what I think of it when I see you next, she laughed. 'Bye."

"Bye" I answered.

I sat staring at the wall in a daze. It was decorated like a sunny summer sky with puffy white clouds drifting across it. My awareness of movement as customers rose from a nearby table brought me out of my reverie. I quickly downed the remains of my coffee and stood to put on my coat which had dried off a bit. A glance at my watch told me that another bus was due in five minutes, so I made my way to the door.

"Bye, Jack. Typical November day out there, eh?" remarked the proprietor.

"It sure is," I replied. "Bye," and I stepped out into the grey, wet afternoon.

I'd just run over to the bus stop, when I realised I'd left the carrier bag on the floor in the café.

"Drat," I muttered and splashed my way back across the road. When I entered the café, I was surprised to see that a young woman was now behind the counter. My glasses immediately steamed up again, but I looked over the top.

"I've left a carrier bag here. I was in just a few minutes ago."

The girl looked blank. "Oh, I don't remember seeing you. Where were you sitting?"

"At that table in the corner," and I turned to point to it. To my astonishment, a couple with a young child and a baby in a high chair were busy eating. It was obvious that they'd been there for some time as there were half-empty plates of food and drinks in front of them. *Whoa!* "I … I'm sure I was sitting there," I stuttered. "There was also a young lady. Wh …where is my bag?" I stood there like a bumbling idiot.

"We've been in here for about half an hour. We haven't seen you," said the young father.

"I think you have made a mistake," decided the girl behind the counter. "Maybe you were in a café further along the street?" she added, trying to be helpful.

"Em … I'm sorry," I blurted and swiftly made my exit. I stood for a moment looking at the café. "It *was* that one," I confirmed to myself. Then I looked up at the name above the window. Quick Stop Snack Bar Sit in or Take Away shone back at me in red lights. There were no other cafes nearby.

Just then, I could see the bus coming and hurried over to the now-crowded shelter.

I sat deep in thought on my homeward journey completely confused by the events of the past half hour. *Had I fallen asleep and dreamt it all? No!*

I'm sure I hadn't. And what about my nephew's present? What happened to that?

When I entered my flat, I shrugged off my coat, hung it up, kicked off my shoes and padded straight to my study. "Hurry up," I exclaimed as I waited for the computer to boot up.

Clicking my way through the formalities, I finally opened the file containing my manuscript. "There it is, *Journey to the Dawn,*" I read aloud.

With a sigh of relief, I pushed my chair away from the desk and wheeled round to my bookshelves. Searching the rows, my eyes alighted on *The Writers and Artists Year Book.* "That's the one!"

I thumbed through the pages until I found the publishing house that had been mentioned at the front of my book. *My book!*

"Can it really be true? Have I somehow been given a glimpse of my future?"

I got up and stalked around the flat. "What if I send my manuscript off to these people?" I walked about with my hands clasped behind my neck. "What if my book *does* get published next year?" I whirled around. "Hell, there's only one way to find out."

I settled back in front of the screen and began to compose an email of introduction to the publisher. When that was completed to my satisfaction, it took only a few moments to attach my synopsis.

"Well, here goes," and I clicked send.

*

Next morning, I awoke with a thick head. My sleep had been disrupted by thoughts of my café visit. *Had I actually bought a present for my nephew and left it in that place? Where was Café Dreams? How could I have jumped forward in time? Had I been a year ahead or just a few months?* So many questions buzzed around.

I had a thought. *I should have the receipt for the Lego set I bought for Josh.* Quickly locating my wallet on the bedside table, I flipped it open to see the folded paper inside. "I knew it! What a relief! I'm not going mad." The receipt clearly showed my purchase. "So, whatever happened to the bag?" I asked aloud.

No answer presented itself.

"Well, I'd better go and buy another Lego set today," I yawned and stretched and made my way to the bathroom.

"All I can do now is wait and see what unfolds," I said to my reflection in the mirror as I shaved. "If the universe has given me the gift of foresight or some such thing, then it will all come about."

I think I'll start popping into that café. If it changes hands and becomes Café Dreams, I'll get really excited. I grinned at the thought. "And there was Claire. Mm. I'd almost forgotten. She was nice," I mused. "Perhaps I'll go in on Fridays. I can always do some people-watching and take some notes in preparation for my next book."

My NEXT book! I laughed aloud and stepped into the shower.

. . .

About the Author

Sheila Caldwell is a retired Holistic Therapist living with her husband in a pretty fishing village in the East Neuk of Fife. She enjoys artwork and writing and takes inspiration from the surrounding area and life experiences.

www.sheilacaldwell.co.uk

Lightning Source UK Ltd.
Milton Keynes UK
UKHW011443130422
401513UK00001B/68